**Dodging into the street,
Scott was hyperfocused on the lovely
but terrified blonde.**

He watched Bree step away from the car with a horrified look on her face.

"Bree!" Scott called.

A car horn screamed.

Brakes squealed.

Scott glanced to his left in time to see a compact car skidding toward him. The driver spun the wheel at the last second and the small car slid past Scott and slammed into a parked car. Scott turned back to the dark sedan, and was about to reach for the door when the driver peeled away, burning rubber on the street.

Without hesitation, he went to Bree and placed gentle hands on her shoulders. "Are you okay?"

She nodded, but he could tell she was traumatized.

"The man in that black car threatened me," she said.

"Threatened you how?"

"He told me to get in, then he flashed a gun."

Scott automatically pulled Bree against his chest into a gentle hug. "It's okay, he's gone."

For now, he added silently.

Books by Hope White

Love Inspired Suspense

Hidden in Shadows
Witness on the Run
Christmas Haven
Small Town Protector
Safe Harbor
* *Mountain Rescue*
* *Covert Christmas*

*Echo Mountain

HOPE WHITE

An eternal optimist, Hope White was born and raised in the Midwest. She began spinning tales of intrigue and adventure when she was in grade school, and wrote her first book when she was eleven—a thriller that ended with a mysterious phone call the reader never heard!

She and her college sweetheart have been married for thirty years and are blessed with two wonderful sons, two feisty cats and a bossy border collie.

When not dreaming up inspirational tales, Hope enjoys hiking, sipping tea with friends and going to the movies. She loves to hear from readers, who can contact her at hopewhiteauthor@gmail.com.

COVERT CHRISTMAS
HOPE WHITE

HARLEQUIN® LOVE INSPIRED® SUSPENSE

Recycling programs
for this product may
not exist in your area.

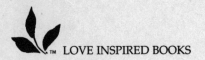 LOVE INSPIRED BOOKS

ISBN-13: 978-0-373-04229-6

Covert Christmas

www.Harlequin.com

Printed in U.S.A.

God is our refuge and strength,
an ever-present help in trouble.
—*Psalms* 46

This book is dedicated to
Washington State Search and Rescue volunteers.
A heartfelt thanks to those who answered my many
questions: Chris, Guy, Bethany and Brenda from
Snohomish County Search and Rescue K9 Unit,
along with Andrew from Everett Mountain Rescue,
and Justin from Bellingham Mountain Rescue.

ONE

They were close, dangerously close.

Scott Becket sprinted up the trail, hoping to disappear in the brush ahead. He wasn't sure how long he could keep up this pace considering the abuse he'd sustained at the hands of his captors. He was lucky to have gotten away, although without his backpack he wouldn't survive long out here in the Cascade Mountains.

Scott needed the perfect spot where he could camouflage himself until they passed, if they passed, because he knew they were nothing if not determined to find Scott and kill him. After they finished what they'd started earlier—"persuading" him to admit where he'd hidden the proof of criminal activity that could destroy them all.

As long as he had sole possession of the documentation, Scott would breathe another day or two, long enough to gather the last bit of evidence he needed to end this thing.

Eyeing the trail ahead, he hoped he wouldn't run into innocent civilians out for an afternoon hike. Scott didn't want to put others in jeopardy and wasn't sure how far his pursuers would go to secure the information and eliminate Scott, the only person cynical enough to question their plan.

He winced at the pain of bruised ribs as he gasped to fill his lungs with air. Scott berated himself for not catching on sooner. What a fool. Just like he'd been a fool to think he could get water samples to the EPA without being caught. But then he hadn't been thinking clearly for a while now.

They'd distracted him with the illusion of love and happiness. Christa had been so good, too, an expert at making him feel safe and loved. He should have known better. Sweet, perfect women like Christa did not fall in love with damaged goods like Scott Becket.

They'd also distracted Scott with threats against his boss and veiled threats against Scott's sister. He hoped Emily took his message seriously and got out of town. If anything happened to his baby sister—

Crack! He ducked at the sound of a gunshot echoing through the woods. Now they were shooting at him? They wouldn't find zip if they killed him first and asked questions later.

He glanced over his shoulder to see how close they were—

His boot hit a tree root sticking up from the trail and he slammed chest-first against the ground, air ripping from his lungs.

It couldn't end like this, with Scott dead in the mountains, the notes and emails he'd collected never making it to the proper authorities.

Junior would continue his plan, and eventually ascend to an even more powerful position as a governor or senator. Scott knew if the guy made it into office people would die from his greed.

Scott scrambled to his feet, his hiking boots getting a solid grip on the soft earth. He wouldn't give up the fight until he was, in fact, dead.

With renewed focus he took off, eyeing a switchback up ahead.

"Stop!" a man shouted.

Sure, stop running and die. Not a chance.

Another *crack* echoed across the mountain range. He hoped someone heard the gunshot and called 9-1-1.

Scott should have called the cops before now, maybe even called his former partner at the Chicago P.D. Right, and have Joe lecture Scott about his screwup with the Domingo kid and subsequent resignation?

Scott didn't have much pull left with law enforcement, which is why being named head of security for Global Resources International had been such a confidence builder.

Or had that been the plan all along, employ a scapegoat like Scott Becket as a fail-safe, someone to take the heat if it all went south?

He hadn't seen it coming.

Approaching another switchback, Scott reached for a tree to steady himself as he made the turn. His momentum put him dangerously close to the edge of the trail overlooking a steep drop. If he could just make it around the corner and out of sight—

Crack!

Pain seared across his upper arm.

He instinctively grabbed it and stumbled,

slipping over the edge and skidding down the lush terrain.

Whack! He came to a sudden stop and gasped for breath. His head throbbed, his arm burned and his ribs ached. He blinked, struggling to focus but his vision wouldn't clear. All he could see was a blur of green above him; all he could hear was the sound of angry voices.

Closer, louder.

A high-pitched ringing cut through the echo of voices.

And darkness consumed him.

Breanna McBride dangled her feet from her position twenty feet up in a tree and gazed at the vast mountain range. The air smelled fresh and invigorating, and the Douglas fir and Western Hemlock scattered across the countryside reminded her that Christmas was only weeks away.

She heard what sounded like a gunshot and wondered if it was a blank fired off to signal the end of the training exercise for the Echo Mountain Search and Rescue K9 unit.

Some might accuse Bree of being overly enthusiastic for hiding out up here; others might call her crazy. But Grace Longfellow, the SAR group leader, asked Bree to plan an exceptional challenge for today's candidates and handlers, so she found this camouflaged spot high off the ground in Woods Pass.

It could happen, Bree mused. A hiker could fall from a trail up above and land in a tree, maybe. Bree figured they should be ready for anything. Today was the final test, the graduation for three more dogs hoping to join the SAR K9 team.

She waited. Turned up the volume on her radio so she wouldn't miss the announcement. The exercise wouldn't have ended until the dogs found Bree, right?

A second shot echoed across the mountains and she ripped her radio off her belt. "This is Bree. Has the training exercise ended, over?"

"We're still looking for you and one other victim, over," Grace answered.

"But I heard—" Sudden movement caught her eye. A body tumbled onto the trail below, landing maybe twenty feet from her tree. "I think we have a real victim, over."

"He's gotta be down there!" a man's voice called from the distance.

Bree raised her lightweight binoculars and spotted two men heading down the trail.

One of them was carrying a gun.

Her heart raced as her mind clicked off possible reasons why a man would be carrying a handgun in the national park. Hunting was illegal here, and the last time someone was shot in the park it was a private investigator shot by a criminal involved in a theft ring.

Bree's eyes darted from the two armed men to the unconscious one on the trail. She was torn between staying concealed and safe or helping him. Maybe if someone would have helped her when she was with her ex-boyfriend Thomas....

"Don't be foolish," she whispered. How could she possibly defend herself and an injured man against two men with guns?

"Grace, I've got a situation here," she said into the radio. "We may need the police. There are two assailants, one is carrying a handgun, and a third man who is wounded, over."

"Location?"

Bree gave her the coordinates. "I'm turning down the radio so they don't hear you."

"Stay hidden," Grace ordered.

"Copy that."

Bree took a slow, deep breath to calm her frantic heartbeat. She hadn't felt this kind of adrenaline rush, this kind of fear since...

"Thomas," she hushed.

No, she'd left that behind when she'd fled Seattle, returned to Echo Mountain and rebooted her life. She thought she'd erased the fear and trepidation from her mind. From her soul.

The wounded man groaned and managed to stand up.

And that's when she saw the blood seeping between his fingers as he gripped his upper arm.

She glanced to her right. The gunmen were heading straight for him. She snapped her attention to the wounded man. He stumbled a few feet....

In the direction of the gunmen!

Her gaze snapped back and forth from the gunmen to the wounded man back to the gunmen. With a groan, the man fell to his knees and collapsed on the ground. Unconscious, exposed and so utterly vulnerable.

"No." She flung her leg over the branch

and climbed down from the tree, unable to sit here and watch a man be brutalized. She had to help him.

She must be out of her mind.

Hitting the ground, she called in. "Grace, the gunmen are headed my way. I need to help the wounded man, over."

"Bree, don't—"

"I can't watch them kill the guy, over."

She turned down the volume on the radio and rushed to the man's side. He was in his thirties with brown hair and a slight beard, and wasn't carrying a backpack. His shirt was ripped in spots and she noticed a nasty gash above his right eye.

She felt for a pulse. Strong and steady.

Now what? The man was solidly built and probably weighed close to two hundred pounds. His pursuers were five, maybe six minutes away.

"Sir, we have to move. Sir?" She gave him a gentle shake.

He opened his eyes. They were a dulled shade of blue that she suspected were more vivid on a normal day.

"I… Emily?" He blinked a confused expression at her.

"Come on, you're not safe here."

She encouraged him to get up and put his arm around her shoulder. Although worried about his blood loss, she couldn't take the time to dress the wound until they were safely out of sight. Bree led him to the edge of the trail where she'd seen a plateau maybe five feet below. She'd noticed it from her spot in the tree, and made a mental note that it would serve as good cover if someone got caught out here in a storm.

She didn't imagine using it to save a man's life.

"We're going to climb down there." She pointed. "Think you can do it?"

He glanced down below, but didn't answer. He seemed out of it. She touched his cheek and his gaze drifted to her eyes.

"Watch me." She shifted onto her belly and grabbed a tree root. "Hold on to this and edge your way down. It's not far."

She dropped onto the plateau and motioned to him. "Your turn."

At first he didn't move. Instead, his gaze drifted across the lush forest in the distance.

"Hey, Blue Eyes." She clapped her hands. He looked at her.

"Come on, buddy. Please?"

He sat down and for a second she thought he'd given up. Instead, he shifted onto his stomach.

"That's it, now grab the tree root—"

He dropped down and wavered. She grabbed his jacket, yanking him away from the ledge.

"Good job," she said, releasing him and taking off her pack.

He leaned against the mountainside and sat down, his eyes half closed, his breathing quick and shallow. She wondered if he were going into shock.

"What's your name?" she whispered, joining him.

"My...name," he said, his eyes drifting shut.

Voices echoed across the canyon. She plastered herself as close to the mountain wall as possible to stay out of sight. The stranger leaned against Bree's shoulder. Concerned that the men above might be able to see his legs sticking out, she encouraged Blue Eyes to sit parallel to the mountain wall, hidden from view. She sat cross-legged, and eased him back to cradle his head in her lap.

She stroked his hairline, assessing his head wound, trying to block out the fear and panic of being discovered.

It was at that moment she realized neither her friends nor police would make it here in time to save them. A familiar knot of helplessness coiled in her stomach.

She was the only one she could depend on, the only one this wounded man could depend on.

No, that wasn't totally true.

Our Father, which art in Heaven, Hallowed be Thy name, she thought, reciting the Lord's Prayer in her head to calm the anxiety threatening to take hold.

This all seemed so surreal, like she was watching someone else go through the motions of climbing out of a safe spot in a tree to help a stranger.

"I won't…" the man whispered. "I won't let them hurt you, Emily."

"Shh," she soothed. She needed him to stay quiet, yet she wondered if the pain from his arm wound or head injury was making him agitated.

"He's here! I know he's here!" a man's voice echoed.

They were getting close.

The gravity of her situation suddenly hit her. The wounded man had been shot in a public park in the middle of the day. These men were brutal killers undeterred by anything or anyone.

Her mind started down that terrifying road, the one that led to panic, so she took a slow deep breath and counted to five. Then exhaled, also counting to five. This wasn't just about Bree protecting herself anymore. This was about a wounded man being hunted like an animal.

With her free hand she fingered the silver locket she had bought with her first check as groundskeeper for Echo Mountain Resort. To Bree the dove engraved on the front not only represented the Holy Spirit, but also freedom, freedom to live her life without the cloak of fear clouding her mind, fear of being hurt, fear of making a mistake.

She hoped this wasn't her biggest mistake, she thought, stroking the blue-eyed man's hair to keep him calm.

"You can't run forever!" a man threatened from above.

Bree stilled. Held her breath.

"He's probably dead," another man with a husky voice said.

"We need proof."

"Forget it. We don't have proper gear to go climbing down mountains."

"Then we'll get gear and come back."

"Are you nuts?" the husky voice challenged. "By tomorrow his body will be torn apart by wild animals. Done."

"He's gonna want proof."

"Wait, what's this?"

Her breath caught in her throat. Had they found something that exposed Bree's hiding place?

"Blood," the husky-voiced man said.

"I told you I nailed him."

"There, it leads over the side."

"You think he's down there?"

Bree closed her eyes and prayed they weren't looking directly down at the plateau. She couldn't be sure that she and Mr. Blue Eyes were completely hidden from view.

"Look down there."

Bree's mind cataloged everything she had in her backpack: water, snacks, compass, map, fire starter, extra clothes and first-aid kit. Wasn't there something she could use to defend herself?

"I don't see anything," the husky voice said.

Blue Eyes groaned, gripping his injured arm.

"Shh," she soothed as best she could, considering the terror filling her chest.

"Did you hear that?"

Silence rang in Bree's ears. She waited. Patted the wounded man's forehead, hoping her touch would soothe him, quiet him.

"You're imagining things," the husky voice said.

"I'm not imagining that blood."

"He went over the edge and hit bottom."

"Or he's right down there."

"Where?"

Bree stilled. They'd figured it out.

With unusual calm, she dug quietly in her pack, her hands searching for something, anything she could use as a weapon.

Rely on yourself and only yourself. That had been her mantra for at least six months following her breakup with Thomas. It had been an isolated existence, but good training for emergency situations.

Like this one.

"You want to go down there and check?" the husky voice said. "Go ahead. I didn't hear anything."

"Then you need to get your hearing checked."

Bree's fingers grazed across her snack bag and water bottle, then brushed across the canister of pepper spray she'd purchased after the mugging.

It was dumb luck that she'd forgotten to take it out of her backpack after moving back to the country. She slipped it out and put her finger on the button.

Calmed her breathing.

Prepared herself for the worst. Although she had martial arts training, this small area wasn't the ideal space to spar with a violent man.

"You got rope?" a male voice said.

"It's not that far," Husky countered. "But I think you're wasting your time."

Bree's pulse sped up. Her heart pounded against her chest.

She could do this. She could defend herself and Mr. Blue Eyes from his attackers.

You naive little country girl, Thomas's words haunted her.

"Emily," Blue Eyes whispered.

"I heard it," Husky said. "Go get him."

Bree held her breath and prayed.

TWO

With a shaky finger on the canister, Bree reminded herself to breathe. Would there be enough pepper spray to immobilize two men if they both came down?

I can do this. I am a strong woman.

The echo of barking dogs sparked relief in Bree's chest. The SAR team was closing in on her location.

"Wait, listen. Dogs, a pack of them," the husky-voiced guy said.

"Wild dogs?"

"No, idiot, search-and-rescue dogs. I saw their van at the trailhead. We've gotta get out of here."

"What about—?"

"Forget it. Let's go."

A few minutes passed, silence ringing in Bree's ears. The gunmen weren't coming down to investigate; she and Blue Eyes were safe for the time being. Now, to make sure he didn't lose too much blood while they waited to be rescued.

The thought snapped her into action. She radioed her position to Grace and dug in her pack for her first-aid kit.

"Grace, the victim will need medical assistance, over," Bree said.

"What's his condition, over?"

"Head injury and gunshot wound. I can deal with the head injury, over."

She pulled out an antiseptic wipe and winced as she cleaned the man's head wound. It was pretty bad and would probably need stitches. In the meantime she applied a butterfly bandage.

His eyes fluttered open. "Who…are you?"

"Breanna, but you can call me Bree."

"Bree…anna," he whispered and his eyes fluttered shut.

"Now comes the hard part," she said to herself. His arm. She'd taken first-aid classes, sure, but a gunshot wound wasn't exactly standard practice.

"Bree, this is Trevor. How's his airway and breathing, over?"

"Seems okay. He's in and out of consciousness. He suffered a head injury, but I'm more worried about the gunshot wound to his arm, over."

"Apply pressure to slow the bleeding," Trevor said. "If it's a through-and-through apply it to both entry and exit wounds. If he goes into shock, cover him up if his skin's cold or remove outer gear if he's hot, over."

"Thanks, over."

"We're a few minutes away. Hang in there, over."

"I'm actually about five feet below the trail, over."

"Copy that," Trevor said.

Bree refocused on tending her patient. She pulled out two spare T-shirts and a scarf. She slid his jacket off, and ripped the material away from his wound, which wasn't as bad as she'd originally thought. It looked as though the bullet had grazed the skin of his upper arm, but didn't pass through his flesh. She wrapped one of the shirts around his arm and secured it with the scarf.

Rinsing blood from her hands with water and antiseptic, she caught herself humming, a coping mechanism she'd developed to stay calm. Only now did she realize what she'd done: saved a man's life, and her own, from armed gunmen.

Up to this point she'd been going through the motions in a detached state, as if she were watching a movie. She'd felt this kind of detachment before. It had been a tool to numb herself to a brutal, violent scene. And there were plenty of those when she'd dated Thomas.

"No reason to think about that," she said, shaking off the unpleasant memories.

Right now, at this moment in time, she was okay, the stranger was relatively okay, and help was close. She could fully freak out and process all this later when she got back to her cottage at the resort.

She pressed the back of her hand against the man's cheek to determine if he was going into shock.

"You're cold, all right." She pulled a thermal blanket out of her pack and covered him up. "Hang in there, buddy. Help's on the way."

The most beautiful sound floated across his mind.

The sound of a woman humming.

She hummed a familiar Christmas song, only he couldn't remember the title. He cracked open his eyes but all he could see through blurred vision was a bright mass of gold.

"Hey there," she said.

He thought she smiled but couldn't tell for sure. Her voice sounded throaty, yet feminine, and he wanted to hear more of it.

"I..." is all he could get out.

"You're going to be okay."

She was wrong, of course. He knew she was wrong, yet he couldn't explain why. They were both in serious danger and had to get out of here.

"Trip..."

"I would have tripped too if I'd been chased by those goons," she said.

"Have to...go." He struggled to sit up but a firm hand pressed against his chest.

A firm, yet calming hand placed directly over his heart. "It's okay. Those guys are gone. We're safe and help is coming."

He believed her. He didn't know why. He was not the type of man to trust easily or believe strangers, especially not a woman.

"What's your name?" she asked.

He blinked a few times, struggling to make her face come into focus.

"My name?" he said.

"I'm Bree, remember?"

He didn't remember Bree, he didn't remember much of anything.

"I can't... Don't remember."

"Not even your name?"

He shook his head, exhaling a quick breath of panic.

"Hey, hey, it's okay. We'll figure it out."

Her soft warm hand stroked his cheek in a soothing gesture. He closed his eyes, fighting to remember who he was, where he was from and why he was here with this woman.

"You've probably got a concussion. With a little time it will come back to you." She ran her fingers down his hairline to his jaw. Once, twice. "It's going to be okay," she whispered.

But it wouldn't be okay, not unless he... What? What was he supposed to do?

Blinking his eyes open, his gaze landed on her smile. His vision was clearing. That had to be a good sign, right? This view was definitely a good thing. A beautiful woman stared down at him, offering a warm and caring smile. She wasn't glamorous like a cover model. She was adorable, a girl-next-door type of beautiful you read about in novels but wondered if they really existed.

"Your eyes look better," she said, withdrawing her hand from his face.

He wanted to beg her to continue the nurturing gesture, but he couldn't bring himself to say the words. Begging a woman for anything felt wrong, and downright stupid.

"I can see you," he said.

"That's awesome. How's the pain on a scale of one to ten?"

"Pain?"

"Your arm, your head?"

"Were we...hiking together?"

"No, I was out here for a search-and-rescue training mission and saw you fall."

"I fell?"

"Yes."

He struggled to remember why he'd come out here in the first place. His gaze drifted beyond the woman to the brilliant shades of green surrounding them. It was so peaceful out here, so serene.

"One to ten?" she prompted.

He redirected his attention to her. "What?"

"Your pain?"

"Seven?"

"There's no wrong answer. Just be honest and it will all work out."

Honest? Was she kidding?

"That bad, huh?" she said.

"What?"

"The pain. You made a face like someone shoved a lemon in your mouth."

"Yeah, I guess it hurts," he said, concerned that she was able to read him so easily.

"Well, it'll probably get worse before it gets better. We're going to have to lift you out of here and carry you down the trail to an ambulance."

"No hospital." He'd be an easy target for sure. But for whom?

"Sorry, Blue Eyes, but a gunshot wound warrants a trip to the E.R., and probably a meet-and-greet from the local police."

"But—"

"Save your strength."

She placed her hand against his chest again, this time gently patting him in a rhythm that soothed him into a state of relaxation. His eyes drifted shut.

* * *

Pain speared down his arm to his fingertips. "Ah, God," he breathed.

But God couldn't help him, not after everything he'd done.

"Take it easy," a woman's stern voice said. "You're hurting him."

It was the blonde from before. What was her name again?

He opened his eyes. Struggled to focus. But everything seemed to bounce around him. The sky, the trees, the blonde beauty.

"Hey, Blue Eyes," she said. "We're almost there."

He wanted to reach out but his arms were bound to a board of some kind. He must have looked panicked because she slid her hand into his and squeezed.

"We had to secure you to the litter so you'd remain as still as possible. We don't want you losing any more blood than necessary. Okay?" She smiled.

"Okay," he thought he said. Closed his eyes. Listened to the conversation around him.

"Why can't they send a helo?" the woman said.

"No place to land up here. The ambulance is waiting," a male voice answered.

"I'm afraid he's losing too much blood."

"His vitals are good."

"Will they—"

"Bree, take a breath. He's alive. You're alive. All is well."

Something pinched his arm. He opened his eyes. "What, ouch."

"Hello, Mr. Smith," a young female paramedic said. "I'll call you Mr. Smith because we couldn't find any identification and it seems more dignified than calling you Mr. Blue Eyes." She sneered at the cute blonde woman standing on the other side of him.

Her name, he desperately needed to remember the blonde's name.

"Are you allergic to any medications?" the paramedic asked.

"I don't…think so."

"Can you tell me what day it is?"

His gazed drifted past her to the lush forest in the distance. They were outside, surrounded by green. How did he get here again?

"Sir?"

He glanced at the paramedic, a twenty-something brunette with a tattoo of a butterfly on her neck. "It's daytime."

"Do you know what day it is?"

He glanced at the blonde beauty. She offered an encouraging smile. It didn't help.

"How about your name?" the paramedic said.

"I told you he doesn't remember," the blonde said with an edge to her voice.

"Sir, do you know where you are?" the paramedic tried again.

"Mountains," he gasped, hating the sound of his voice. Weak. Defeated.

"What city or state?" she asked, administering something into his IV.

"I… Washington?"

The blonde beauty offered a bright smile. He could look at those green eyes, that joyful smile all day long.

"Do you remember the trailhead or mountain you went climbing this morning?"

He glanced at the blonde. She started to mouth something.

"Bree!" the EMT scolded. "No cheating."

"Sorry." Bree put up her hands.

Bree, that's right. A charming name.

"Okay, let's get you into the ambulance." The paramedic nodded at someone behind him. The stretcher shifted slightly, then he was lifted up into the ambulance.

"Bree," he said, panicked. He reached out hoping to touch her again, feel her calming presence.

"It's okay. I'll meet you at the hospital," she said.

He may not make it to the hospital. He didn't know the brunette with the butterfly tattoo. He didn't trust her.

"Bree." He struggled to sit up.

"Easy there, Mr. Smith. You don't want to pull out your IV."

"Bree," he croaked, desperate, trying to roll off the stretcher.

Suddenly she was beside him, holding his hand.

"Right there is fine," the paramedic ordered Bree, then said to the driver, "Okay, Roscoe, let's go."

He turned his head to the left, needing to see Bree, look into her green eyes. Green like the forest. Her image started to blur again. He was losing focus, losing consciousness.

"I can't… Bree…"

He closed his eyes, but felt her squeeze his hand.

"What's happening to him?" she asked.

"It's probably the pain meds," the paramedic said.

"But he should stay conscious, shouldn't he? Especially if he has a head injury?"

"Calm down, cuz. He's stable. It's all good."

He was drifting in and out, picking up only pieces of conversation.

I couldn't let him die.

Two gunmen?

He wasn't with them; they were after him.

That was foolish.

I don't care. He needed me.

You don't even know him.

He squeezed her hand, struggling to stay connected, to stay conscious.

"It's okay," a woman whispered against his ear.

It was Bree's voice. He'd know it anywhere.

He couldn't remember his own name, where he'd been or how he'd ended up in an ambulance. Those three things should drive him to the brink of despair.

But they didn't because Bree was here. He took a deep breath, clung to her hand and drifted.

"You've upset him," Bree snapped at her cousin Maddie.

"Right, so it's not the bullet wound or head injury that's got him freaked out," Maddie said, sarcastically. "Look, I shouldn't have let you ride along in the first place, so stop busting my chops."

"I'm worried about him." She noted Mr. Blue Eyes' skin looked pale.

"He's not your problem."

Bree ignored the comment and stroked the back of his hand.

"Bree?"

She glanced at her cousin, who frowned with concern.

"You didn't see him, Maddie. He was so—" Bree glanced at the bruise forming around his head wound "—broken."

Maddie reached over and touched Bree's shoulder. "I'm sorry."

With a nod, Bree glanced back at the stranger. They both knew Maddie's words referred more to Bree's terrible Thomas past than the current situation.

"He's okay," Maddie said, pausing as she unbuttoned his shirt. "Whoa."

"What?"

"He's got a lot of redness on his chest and stomach, like he was beaten up."

They pulled up to the hospital.

"This is as far as you go, sorry," Maddie said.

The back door opened. Two sheriff's deputies stood there, along with Echo Mountain Police Chief Lew Washburn, and Wallace Falls Police Chief Charles Trainer, who Bree's family fondly called Uncle Chuck.

Two officers and two police chiefs? Blue Eyes must be in big-time trouble.

"Bree," he groaned, opening his eyes.

Maddie shot Bree a disapproving look.

"I'm here," Bree said, squeezing his hand.

The other paramedic came around and helped Maddie lift the stretcher out of the ambulance. Blue Eyes didn't release Bree's hand.

Uncle Chuck approached. "Breanna, we need to—"

"I'll be right back," she interrupted.

She walked alongside the stretcher, offering words of comfort to Blue Eyes. "You'll be okay. They'll take care of you here."

"Don't leave."

"I'll stay close, promise."

"You've got to let him go, Bree," Maddie said as they wheeled him into the E.R.

Bree released his hand.

"No, Bree," he gasped, and the look in his eyes nearly tore her apart inside. Pure and utter devastation coupled with fear. She'd seen that look…in the mirror.

She motioned for her cousin to stop the stretcher and Bree leaned close to the stranger. "I'll be right outside. Let them fix you up so you can get out of here and do something fun."

"With you?"

Bree shot a quick glance at Maddie and looked back at the stranger. "Sure."

"You won't leave me?"

"I won't leave you."

He released her hand and they wheeled him into the examining area. Bree automatically reached for her locket, praying for guidance. Had she done the right thing by making that promise? Of course she had, because it had calmed him down enough to release her and get much needed medical attention.

"Breanna?"

She turned to Uncle Chuck and Chief Washburn.

"Hey, hi, Uncle Chuck." She gave him a hug. Chuck had been a friend for years and helped out after Dad had passed away.

They broke the hug and she nodded at Lew Washburn. "Hey, Chief."

"Let's sit down and you can give me your official statement." Chief Washburn motioned her to the waiting area.

Breanna hesitated, not wanting to break her word to Blue Eyes.

"We'll be close to the examining room," Chief Washburn said.

With a nod, Breanna accompanied them to the waiting area, positioning herself so she could keep an eye on the door.

"Do you know the victim?" Uncle Chuck asked her.

"No." Although she felt oddly connected to him in a way she couldn't explain.

"Tell us what happened," Chief Washburn said.

As Bree retold the story, she clicked into that distancing mode, the place where it felt as if she was talking about someone else.

"You jumped out of the tree to help him, knowing he was being pursued by two gunmen?" Uncle Chuck said.

She didn't miss the disbelief in his voice, nor the disapproval.

"They would have killed him," she said.

"They might have killed you," he scolded.

His tone sparked shame through her body, but she pushed it aside. She would not feel ashamed for saving a man's life.

"They were far enough away that I didn't feel I was in immediate danger," she said. "I thought I had enough time to help the man hide until authorities arrived."

"When I tell your mother—"

"Please let me do it. I'll call her as soon as we're done."

Bree surely didn't want people tattling on her, although considering how many people had probably heard about the morning's events, Bree suspected Mom already knew. Small towns were like that.

"What else can I tell you?" She directed her question to Chief Washburn.

"A description of the gunmen."

She described what they looked like, trying to recall details from when she viewed them through the binoculars.

"One of the men said 'he's gonna want proof,'" Bree said.

"You were so close that you could hear what they were saying?" Uncle Chuck's voice pitched.

"Uncle Chuck, I've been through a traumatic event. It's just now hitting me how dangerous it was and you're not helping."

"I'm sorry, you're right, I'm sorry."

But it was natural for him to worry. He was protective of the McBride clan.

"Let's all take a breath," Chief Washburn said. "Breanna's okay, but we have two gunmen on the loose and we need to involve as many law enforcement personnel as possible to track them down so no one else gets hurt."

"They had accents," Bree said.

"Foreign or...?" Chief Washburn asked.

"Midwest, Chicago. You know that nasal A sound?"

"Okay, that's good." The chief wrote something in his notepad. "As I understand it, there was no ID on the victim?"

"That's right."

"Did he tell you his name?" Chief Washburn asked.

"He doesn't seem to remember it."

"Convenient," Uncle Chuck muttered.

"He's got a nasty head wound," she said defensively.

The E.R. doors opened to the outside and she spotted a familiar group of people: the SAR K9 team, along with Bree's brother, Aiden, and their mom. So much for Bree calmly breaking the news to Mom about today's events. Bree's best friend, Billie, and her fiancé, Quinn, were also with the group.

Aiden marched up to Bree, who put out her hand in a stop gesture. "I'm fine, but I need another minute to give my statement."

She didn't miss Mom's worried frown, or the angry twist of Aiden's mouth. He'd better not be angry with her or she'd let him have it. Bree had been holding it in these past few hours, trying to remain calm and levelheaded for Blue Eyes. It wouldn't take much for her to lose her cool, especially with family who she knew loved her no matter how cranky she got.

Bree finished describing the two men. Chief Washburn asked, "About the gunshot victim, any idea who he is or why he was assaulted?"

"No, sir. He didn't say much, although he said a name, Emily, and that he'd keep her safe."

The chief jotted something down. "Did he have a backpack?"

"No, sir. Maddie the EMT made a comment about his chest and torso looking red, too, like he'd been beaten up."

"And he said nothing that would give us a clue what he was doing out on the trail?"

"No, sorry."

"It seemed like he's bonded with you," Chief Washburn said.

Mom and Aiden were within earshot, but she didn't care. "Yes, sir, I believe he has."

"He trusts you?" Chief Washburn said.

"He's scared. He can't remember anything, even his name, and he's in a strange hospital with multiple injuries. He needs to trust someone."

"And you're okay with that?" Chief Washburn said.

"Yes, sir."

"Even though this could be a dangerous man?"

"We don't know that."

"Someone was shooting at him," Uncle Chuck interjected.

"I know," she said, glancing at him, "I was there, remember?"

Bree wasn't usually a smarty-pants, but she was tired of people passing judgment on her. They'd passed judgment on her relationship with Thomas, which is one of the reasons she'd stayed silent about the emotional abuse for so long.

A few people had also given her a hard time about no longer doing hair when she'd moved back to town, instead choosing to be a groundskeeper, working for her brother who managed Echo Mountain Resort. Everyone seemed to have an opinion about Bree's life. Some days she wished they'd all spend their energy worrying about themselves.

"I can't make any sense out of your behavior today," Chuck said.

"Why don't you go check on Margaret?" Chief Washburn suggested to Uncle Chuck.

Chuck had obviously lost objectivity in regards to this situation because of how much he cared about Bree's mom. It was the worst kept secret in town.

Chief Washburn closed his notebook. "I'm going to assign an officer to watch over the victim. I'm sure your family is going to encourage you to detach from this situation."

"I can't," she said.

"Because?"

"I feel a connection to him."

Chief Washburn studied her and waited for more.

"I know what it's like to feel lost and vulnerable," she said, "to feel so scared and there's no one to help you. I've been there."

"Well, truth is your connection to this man could be my best lead, but I won't be responsible for stirring up trouble between you and your family. If you stick close to him and discover anything that might help with my investigation, please call me." The chief handed her a business card with his office and cell numbers.

"Of course."

He hesitated before standing. "Breanna, you are a remarkably brave woman."

"Thank you, sir."

She glanced past him at the group of family and friends in the waiting area. They probably wouldn't call her brave or applaud her decision to help the stranger.

Bree had survived a violent event, yet had kept it together long enough to give her statement to police. She needed time alone to regroup, a few minutes to let the reality of her situation wash over her—but in private so she wouldn't get emotional in front of her family.

"Hey, Chief, I need to use the washroom. Would you mind telling my family I'll be right back?"

"Sure."

Bree slipped away, hurried down the hall into the single-stall bathroom and locked the door.

She was okay; everything was fine. She studied her reflection in the mirror. The chief would circulate a description of the attackers, and Blue Eyes would get his memory back and help them figure out why someone had tried to kill him.

No matter what her family said, she knew in her heart she'd done the right thing by helping him. She wouldn't allow her overly protective brother to make her feel guilty or ashamed by her actions.

Splashing cool water on her face, Bree considered the words she'd spoken to Blue Eyes. *I'll stay close, promise.*

Maybe she shouldn't have said that, but she desperately wanted him to get medical attention and it seemed as though promising to stay close was the only way to make that happen.

"Looks like I'm hanging around for a while," she whispered to herself, because Bree didn't break promises, even to strangers.

This should be fun, explaining to her family and friends why she was sticking close to a man she barely knew. Make that a man she didn't know at all, heck, she didn't even know his name.

She pulled her hair back, spread gloss on her dry lips and applied a little blush to look healthy, not exhausted. They'd be waiting and wanting details, a reason as to why she'd jump into the midst of gunfire. The only explanation she could offer was that it was the right thing to do.

"Don't second-guess yourself," she said to her reflection in the mirror. That behavior had gotten her into trouble before.

She grabbed her pack and left the bathroom. As she ambled down the hall, she took a deep breath and touched her necklace for strength.

Her family and friends were passionate about keeping her safe because they loved her.

Love, a complicated emotion.

She glanced up and noticed a man leave the E.R. examining room heading in her direction. Boy, it was busy tonight at the Echo County E.R.

She politely smiled at the man as he passed, and he nodded in return. Distracted by thoughts of defending herself from her family, it took a few seconds before she realized he looked familiar.

"I was about to come find you," Aiden said, walking up to her.

In a flash it hit her: the man she just passed was one of the gunmen.

And he'd come out of the examining area where they'd taken Blue Eyes.

"No, no, no," she muttered, shoving her brother aside.

"Bree?"

She rushed past him and flung open the doors to the examining area. The curtains were pulled back and all the beds were empty.

THREE

"Can I help you?" a nurse asked Bree from the corner of the room.

"A man was brought in, thirties, dark hair, blue eyes, slight beard."

"Mr. Smith?"

"Yes, where is he?"

"They moved him."

"Bree, what are you doing?" Aiden said, following her into the examining area.

She turned to him. "Is Chief Washburn still here?"

"Yes, he's—"

"Go tell him I just saw one of the shooters."

"He's here? Are you sure?" Aiden's face reddened.

"Yes, go."

Bree turned back to the nurse and focused on speaking as calmly as possible as she fought the panic building in her chest. "Mr.

Smith's in danger. You need to tell the police where he's been moved so they can protect him."

"Sure, okay, let me check the computer." She went to a terminal and tapped on the keyboard.

"Did anyone else ask about him?" Bree pressed.

"I don't think so, but I just got here."

Chief Washburn rushed into the examining area. "Where did you see him?"

"He passed me in the hallway just now," Bree said.

"Description?"

"Black jacket, maroon shirt. It was the older one, in his sixties, with salt-and-pepper hair, wearing a blue baseball cap with a red *C* on it." Bree shook her head in frustration. "I smiled at him because I didn't realize who he was at first."

"That's a good thing," the chief said. "He won't know we're onto him, and he won't suspect that you recognized him."

The chief spoke into the radio on his shoulder, giving instructions to his officers. He glanced at the nurse, "Room number?"

"Still checking."

"Are you done with my sister, Chief, because I'd like to take her home," Aiden said.

"I can't leave," she said.

"Breanna—"

"They moved him to room 214 on the second floor." The nurse interrupted Aiden.

"Closest stairs?" the chief said.

"Around the corner on the left," the nurse said.

Bree started to go with him, but the chief blocked her. "Please stay with your family where it's safe."

"I have to make sure he's okay."

"That's our job." He nodded at Aiden. "Take her to the waiting area, but don't leave the hospital."

"Yes, sir."

The chief spoke orders into his radio as he rushed out of the examining area. The doors closed behind him and Bree fingered her necklace.

"Hey," Aiden said.

She glanced at him.

"Mom's freaking out. You should probably…" He motioned toward the waiting area.

With a nod, she went to the door and pushed it open, facing her family and friends. Mom rushed to her and offered a loving hug, holding on as if she feared Bree might disappear. Understandable given Bree's history. It had been almost two years since she had abruptly packed up and moved to the city on a quest for more excitement in her life. She had learned the hard way that excitement was overrated.

"I'm okay, Mom." Bree broke the hug and squeezed Mom's hands. "Really, I'm good."

As the rest of the group started firing off questions, Bree put up her hand to silence them.

"I appreciate your support, especially you guys." She nodded at the SAR K9 team members who'd come to the hospital: Grace, Trevor, Christopher and Luke.

"Bree, what happened?" Bree's best friend, Billie, asked with worry in her eyes.

As Bree described the events of the past few hours, she watched her family and friends' expressions change from disbelief to shock to concern.

"She did a brave thing," Trevor offered.

"A potentially deadly brave thing," Aiden said.

Tears welling in her eyes, Mom studied her daughter like she'd never seen her before.

Billie gave Bree a hug. "Quinn and I are headed to California on business tomorrow, but I think I should stay and keep you company."

"No, don't you dare stay back on my account. I'm fine."

"That's debatable," Aiden muttered.

"What do you mean?" Mom said.

Aiden narrowed his eyes at Bree, probably expecting her to confess she'd developed an unhealthy and inappropriate connection to a stranger with a gunshot wound.

"I'm okay," Bree confirmed. "No injuries."

"Good, then we can go home," Mom said, reaching out to take her hand.

"I can't leave the hospital," Bree said.

"Why not?" Mom asked.

"Here we go," Aiden muttered.

"Chief Washburn asked me to stay, and even if he hadn't, I want to be here for Mr. Smith when he wakes up."

"Breanna—"

"Mom, he has no one, no friends, no family here at the hospital. He doesn't even remember who he is. I was able to comfort him and he needs me."

"You don't even know him," Aiden snapped.

"That doesn't make his pain any less real," Bree countered.

"This isn't your responsibility."

"No one should be so scared and alone."

"Are we still talking about that guy or you?" Aiden accused.

"Aiden, that's enough," Mom said.

He planted his hands on his hips and glanced at the floor, shaking his head.

"Breanna is right. The stranger has no one." Mom scanned the group of friends surrounding them. "We have the wonder of love and friendship." Mom cracked a proud, gentle smile at Bree. "And the Lord would want us to share our gift."

Surrounded by gray, floating in a mass of nothingness, he couldn't be sure he heard the voice. Where was he again?

I'm going to kill you, slowly, painfully.

An inferno of panic exploded in his chest, the pressure causing him to gasp for air. He wanted to call out but could barely stay focused, much less shout for someone to help him.

I'll beat you until you give it up, the voice threatened.

He struggled to form words, willing his vocal cords to kick into gear. If only he could get his mind to grab on to something other than the paralyzing anxiety coursing through him.

Then I'll smother you with a pillow.

"Can I help you?" a woman's voice said.

The blonde woman? Right, because he'd made her promise to stay close. No, please God, this couldn't be her. If the man threatened to suffocate him with a pillow he'd surely have no problem hurting the woman.

The woman? Bree. That was her name.

"Bree," he gasped, remembering her beautiful green eyes, her grounding smile.

A hand gripped his fingers and squeezed. "I'm here."

No, she shouldn't be here. His attacker was close, in the room, poised to smother and kill him. Which put Bree in the way because she was tending to him, holding his hand. He tried to pull away, wanting to let her go so she'd be safe.

"What is it?" she said.

He opened his eyes and she came into focus, her sparkling emerald eyes and heart-shaped face framed with golden hair.

"Danger," he rasped.

"It's okay. There's no danger."

"He said...was going to...kill me."

"No one's here but me." She glanced above him. "And the nurse."

He shifted his head to the side and spotted a brown-haired nurse fiddling with a machine beside his bed. She smiled down at him.

"See, you're A-okay," Bree said.

He turned back to Bree. "He was here."

"In your room?"

He nodded.

She exchanged a glance with the nurse.

"I'll go get the officer," the nurse said.

He didn't take his eyes off Bree. "Officer?"

"A police officer was assigned to your room last night because I saw one of the shooters."

"In my room? You were here when he...?" His voice cracked before he could finish.

"It's okay." She stroked his arm with one hand while still holding onto him with her other. "He passed me in the hallway, that's all." She offered a tender smile. "Are you sure you saw him in here?"

"I heard him."

"He threatened you?" she said.

He nodded.

"I'm so sorry." She sighed. "That must have been terrifying."

Not as terrifying as the thought of the guy hurting Bree.

He was suffering a major head injury all right. Why else would he be more concerned with this woman's well-being than his mission? His mission, which was what again? He couldn't remember. He wasn't even sure how he'd ended up in the hospital.

"What's wrong?" she asked, as if she sensed his anxiety.

"I don't remember how I got here or, sorry, but I don't remember how I know you."

"You don't remember being shot?"

He shook his head.

"Do you remember your name?"

"Scott."

"Nice to meet you, Scott," she said with a relieved smile.

He wondered why she cared so much about him.

A police officer marched up to his bedside. "Ma'am, I should be asking the questions."

"Of course, sorry." She didn't move, still clinging to Scott's hand.

"If you wouldn't mind," the officer said, and motioned for her to leave.

"I don't, go ahead and ask your questions."

The cop narrowed his eyes at her in frustration. "Breanna."

"Ryan," she challenged back.

The cop shook his head, figuring he'd lost this round, and refocused on Scott.

"Sir, I'm Officer McBride with the Echo Mountain P.D. I've been assigned to keep you in protective custody tonight. Would you mind answering some questions to help us with the investigation?"

"Very professional, A plus," Bree teased.

Officer McBride glared at her.

"Sure," Scott said, trying to shift up in bed.

Bree released his hand and adjusted his pillow behind his back. When she sat back down, he automatically reached for her hand, he wasn't sure why, and she gave it willingly. That got another narrowing of eyes from Officer McBride.

"Let's start with your name," the cop asked, pulling out a small notebook.

"Scott, Scott..." He hesitated. A voice in his head warned that sharing his last name would put him in more danger. "I don't know, Scott something."

"Age?"

"Thirty-one."

"Your occupation?"

"I'm..." He wracked his brain, searching for work or even family-related memories. "I'm a cop," he said, but it didn't feel right. "I think."

"You're not sure?"

"No sir."

"Where do you live?"

"A big city. Detroit? Chicago?"

"What brought you to Echo Mountain?"

"I needed to..."

They would die. He needed to save them.

"I don't remember." He closed his eyes.

He felt Bree squeeze his hand in a supportive gesture, but he couldn't look at her without feeling the shame of failure. Was she one of the people who would die because he couldn't see this through to the end?

"Scott?" the cop said.

He opened his eyes.

"What *do* you remember?"

An image flashed across his mind of a teenager splayed on the ground clinging to a flashlight.

"I don't…" He shook his head. "I'm not sure."

"Anything could help."

"It's all jumbled."

"Do you remember being chased in the mountains?"

"I think so."

He remembered being chased but couldn't be sure if it was a recent memory or a distant one.

"Why do you think those men were chasing you?"

"I don't know."

"You didn't have any identification on you. Did they take it?"

"I guess."

"You sustained trauma to the torso area. Do you remember them assaulting you?"

"I…" He caught glimpses, flashes of images.

"Scott, why did they shoot you?"

"Enough, Ryan," Bree snapped. "You're upsetting him."

"It's my job to get answers, Breanna."

"Well, he's obviously not up to giving you answers, so back off."

"I'm calling the chief." He turned and walked out.

"You do that," she muttered.

It was like they were ten-year-olds fighting over the last peanut butter cookie. A rush of memories filled his thoughts. Scott cracked a smile. They reminded him of he and Emily when they were kids, always competing with one another.

"What's so funny?" she challenged.

"You guys remind me of me and my sister."

"Hey, you remembered something, that's great."

"Yeah, memories from twenty years ago," he said. "So what's the deal with you and the cop?"

"Ryan practically grew up at our house, so he's more like a brother than a cousin. And one thing I do not need is another overly protective brother-type in my life."

"It's not their fault."

She cocked her head in question.

"There's something about you that makes us want to take care of you."

"Well, you shouldn't. I've taken karate and carry a wicked can of pepper spray in my bag, police grade." She cocked her chin.

Yet he sensed trepidation behind her confident words.

"Can I ask you something?" he said.

"Sure."

"Why are you here?"

"Do you want me to leave?"

"No, of course not. I'm just trying to figure out how I got so lucky."

"You were shot, sustained a concussion and bruised ribs. What's so lucky about that?"

"The fact that a beautiful woman is sitting beside my bed."

She blushed and glanced at their hands. "You're embarrassing me."

"Sorry, it was meant to be a compliment." Scott didn't remember a lot, but he knew that most women appreciated compliments.

Wasn't it obvious Bree wasn't "most" women?

"How's Mr. Smith?" a doctor said, coming into the room.

"Actually, he remembered his name," Bree offered.

"Excellent." The doctor extended his hand to Bree. "I'm Dr. Vann and you are who, his girlfriend?"

"No." She blushed again. "Just a friend."

She looked even more adorable when she blushed. Scott's chest ached with wanting something he could never have—a gentle, nurturing woman like Bree in his life.

"Let's take a look." Dr. Vann flashed a penlight in Scott's eyes and examined his head wound. "Head injuries are tricky. I suspect you're suffering from retrograde amnesia, a condition where a patient forgets the events preceding and immediately following the head injury. The severity of the injury will affect how far back you can remember. Do you recall what happened leading up to your injury?" The doctor jotted something on a clipboard.

"No, sir," Scott answered.

"What is the last thing you *do* remember?"

A memory sparked in his mind of he and his partner, Joe, interviewing a witness. "I remember a case I was working on."

"And when was that?"

"I'm not sure."

"Do you know why you're in the hospital?" the doctor asked.

"Someone shot me."

"So, you remember the shooting?"

"Not really."

Dr. Vann glanced at Scott.

"I told him what happened," Bree said.

"We should probably let him remember on his own," the doctor said.

"Oh, okay, sorry."

Scott did not want her feeling badly because of him and he knew the sooner he got out of here and away from Bree, the safer she'd be. "How long do I have to stay in the hospital?"

"Overnight to keep an eye on the head injury." Dr. Vann glanced at a pager on his belt. "I'll check in later. The best thing for the patient is rest." The doctor nodded at Bree and left the room.

A phone vibrated in Bree's pocket and she pulled it out, glanced at the text and frowned.

"You need to go," Scott said. "It's okay."

"It's not critical. It's my brother pulling his boss card to get me away from," she hesitated, "the hospital."

"You mean away from me?" He cracked a half smile.

"Pretty much. Don't take it personally. The perks of having an overprotective family."

"Sounds nice." And it did, especially since he'd grown up in a single parent household with a mom who had to work two jobs to support Scott and his sister. There had been no extended family, no protective adults to keep an eye on Scott and Emily.

He suddenly grew tired and couldn't hold back a yawn.

"I should let you sleep," she said.

"Okay," he said, but he didn't let go of her hand. His eyes drifted shut and his mind wandered, his imagination landing on a peaceful, majestic view of a valley from the top of a mountain.

And beside him stood the adorable Breanna with the enchanting smile.

Bree decided to spend the night at the hospital. Her family and friends followed Mom's lead and supported Bree's decision to help the stranger. Once the police determined the gunman was no longer in the hospital, Bree sent everyone home while she hovered at Scott's bedside. She was even able to convince Aiden to feed and walk Bree's dog, Fiona, but not without a lecture.

At first Bree wasn't sure hospital staff would let her hang out all night, but Chief Washburn said it was okay and left 24-hour police protection outside Scott's room. Bree felt safe and was where she needed to be— beside Scott's bed.

When they'd come in to check his vitals he'd wake up with a panicked look, asking where he was and what had happened. Bree would tell him he was safe, everything was okay, and he'd drift back to sleep.

But morning came and Aiden demanded she show up at work by noon or find another job. It was an empty threat, of course, but she respected his position and did as ordered, leaving Scott alone. She hoped he'd sleep most of the day to give his body a chance to heal.

She didn't like being away from Scott, but couldn't rationalize blowing off an entire day of work to babysit a grown man, a stranger. Still, when she thought about the vulnerable look on his face she knew she'd get back to the hospital. She only wished it was earlier than eight in the evening.

Thanks to big brother Aiden, she had extra holiday lights to string along the split rail fence bordering Resort Drive. No surprise that he'd told the other part-timers to go home at three because he was watching his payroll numbers.

Truth was, he was doing his best to keep her busy and away from the hospital. Since Aiden was tied up with a guest when it was time for her to leave, she avoided lecture number seven, or was it seventeen?

Pulling into the hospital lot, she parked near an overhead light and glanced out her window before getting out of the car. She hoped tonight's staff knew she was on the list of people allowed to come by after visiting hours.

As she marched across the lot, she started to wonder if everyone was justified in worrying about her attachment to Scott. She didn't have the best track record with romantic relationships; make that a dismal track record.

But this wasn't about romance, it was about helping someone in need, a man she felt a visceral connection to when she looked into his wary eyes.

She rode the elevator to the second floor and when she got out she noticed the absence of a police officer outside of Scott's room. She fought the panic ringing in her ears. Perhaps Scott had remembered something and the officer on duty was in his room taking his statement.

Her pulse quickened as she stepped into the doorway. "Scott?"

The bed was empty.

"Can I help you?" a nurse said coming down the hall.

"Scott's gone" was all Bree could get out.

"Are you a relative?"

"Where is he?"

"A police officer took him away."

"Took him where?"

"I'm assuming to lockup. He was arrested."

FOUR

"Arrested?" Bree said. "How long ago did they leave?"

"Maybe ten minutes?"

"Where were they taking him?"

"I'm not sure."

Bree spun around and rushed toward the stairs. As she passed the elevators, the doors opened and her cousin Ryan marched out. Bree hesitated.

"Why did the police arrest Scott?" she asked.

"What are you talking about? I was sent to relieve Officer Waters."

"Then Waters arrested him?"

"No one arrested him that I know of."

"He's gone, Ryan. The nurse said he was arrested."

"That's not right." Ryan motored to the room as if he couldn't comprehend Bree's words. When he spotted the empty bed, he shot her a concerned frown and pressed the button on his shoulder radio. "This is Officer McBride. Where did Officer Waters take Scott Smith, over?"

Bree and Ryan stared at each other, both dreading the response about to come through the radio. Was this a mix-up or had something nefarious happened?

"Officer Waters said he was relieved twenty minutes ago by a sheriff's deputy, over."

Ryan went to the nurse's station. "Who authorized the patient in room 214 to be released into police custody?"

The two nurses turned to the doctor standing behind them.

"Not me," the doctor said.

"Please check the patient's chart," Ryan said, calmly.

The redheaded nurse typed something into the computer. A few nerve-racking seconds passed, then she said, "Dr. Vann released him."

"Please page him for me," Ryan instructed the redheaded nurse.

Bree turned and headed for the elevators.

"Where are you going?" Ryan called after her.

She shook her head, frustrated.

"Stay out of this, Bree."

Man, she was tired of people telling her what to do. Ever since the Thomas trauma people treated her like a fragile doll, breakable by the slightest touch.

The elevator doors opened but she decided she needed to walk instead and took the stairs. She was worried, beyond worried, suspecting that whoever was after Scott in the mountains had managed to kidnap him from the hospital to finish what they'd started.

Or was she overreacting because she'd developed an unhealthy attachment to the stranger with the striking blue eyes? She got to the ground floor and was about to open the door to the main hallway, when she heard a voice drift up from the basement level. She leaned against the railing, but couldn't see the source of the voice.

"I got him released, but he was fighting it. I couldn't overmedicate him or he wouldn't be able to walk out on his own.... No one is in delivery at this time of night. It's fine."

Bree stepped back, whipped open the door and took off into the hospital. She spotted an orderly.

"Delivery entrance?" she asked.

"Why do you want to know?"

She didn't have time for a lengthy discussion so she rushed past him and found a map on the wall. Pausing long enough to figure out the location of the delivery entrance, she ripped her phone out of her pocket and called her cousin Ryan. It went into voice mail. He probably kept the ringer off during his shift. She hung up, fearing by the time he got her voice mail it would be too late.

Scott would be gone, maybe even dead.

Her phone vibrated. Ryan was calling her back.

"They took him out the delivery entrance," she said, without waiting for him to speak. "I'm headed there now."

"No, Bree, don't—"

She ended the call and focused on getting to the entrance and…and…what? Once again she was throwing herself into a potentially dangerous situation in order to save Scott. Mom would be upset; Aiden would be furious. What was Bree supposed to do, let the gunman kidnap Scott against his will?

The mystery voice, which she suspected was Dr. Vann, said Scott was fighting his captor. Good, that meant they might not have left the hospital. She hoped. She prayed.

She got to the delivery area and flung open the door. A long storage aisle led to a dock where they dropped off supplies for the hospital. She yanked a fire extinguisher off the wall as a weapon, and rushed to the end of the dock.

Heart racing, she peered across the back lot into the woods bordering the hospital. She saw nothing, heard no one.

She was too late.

"Scott!" she cried.

Two police cars, lights flashing, sped into the lot.

"Breanna," her cousin said, coming up behind her. "You should have stayed back."

"He's gone," she said, looking into Ryan's brown eyes. "They got him, and they're going to kill him."

He glanced down at her hand, her fingers digging into his arm, then back at her face. "We'll find him."

"Officer McBride!" one of the cops called.

Bree and Ryan both glanced at him. He held up what looked like a hospital ID bracelet. "Found this at the edge of the woods."

"Stay here," Ryan said.

He went to help the other two officers search the surrounding woods. She put down the fire extinguisher and paced, fretted and nibbled her fingernail. Not able to stand it any longer, she hopped down to aid in the search.

"Breanna, I said get back," Ryan ordered.

She froze, but didn't retreat. She needed to be close in case they found Scott. They had to find him or else that meant…

She struggled to calm her breathing, the sound of silence ringing in her ears as she watched them fan out to search the perimeter.

"I've got blood here," one of the officers announced. "It leads this way."

Without waiting for permission, she took off into the woods.

"Bree!" her cousin called.

Scott collapsed in a pile of wet brush and gasped for air. The guy had convinced everyone, including Scott, that he was a legitimate deputy responsible for bringing Scott in for questioning.

Only when they got to the guy's car did Scott suspect something was off. Way off. The supposed deputy had parked in a dark corner of the back lot as if he didn't want to be seen. Through somewhat blurred vision, Scott realized he wasn't getting into a typical cruiser but a rented, high-end luxury vehicle.

Wrong. There's no way a county deputy or small-town P.D. would spring for such an expensive car. Scott got into the back and when the "deputy" slid behind the wheel, Scott darted out the other side, racing for the woods.

The lush evergreens seemed close one minute and miles away the next.

The fake deputy caught up to him and they struggled, but Scott managed to nail him with an uppercut that brought the guy down. Scott sprinted as fast as his exhausted body could take him, deep into the dark woods where he could hide from his kidnapper. He assumed it was one of the guys from yesterday, one of the guys Bree had told him about, but didn't know for sure.

Scott couldn't remember much about the past few days or months, except for the obvious: he'd gotten himself into a world of trouble.

As he stumbled through the woods, he barely felt the branches scraping his cheeks and hands as he forged ahead into the mass of trees.

He staggered to a downed tree trunk, climbed over it and collapsed on the other side, using it for cover. He hated this, hated hiding like a coward, but with his limited brain function he'd be stupid to go on the offensive. Instead, he'd hide out and wait. For what, to be rescued?

Not likely. He was rescued yesterday by the adorable blonde and her friends but no one was lucky enough to be rescued twice in two days. He closed his eyes, waiting for the inevitable, trying to think of another strategy to buy himself a little more time.

Time to finish something important, but what?

He heard the crunch of footsteps against fallen twigs as his attacker closed in. Scott was going to die. The man had said as much when he'd threatened him in the hospital.

Scott.

But it was *her* voice, the beautiful, gentle voice that awakened him yesterday, calmed him when he thought he'd go mad. In his last minutes on earth he was hallucinating, hearing the gentle voice of Breanna calling out to him.

"Scott!" Her voice carried across the dense forest.

He blinked open his eyes. It wasn't a dream.

"I'm here," he croaked, his voice raw and weak.

"Did you hear that?" a man said.

Scott shrank lower into the earth. Maybe her voice wasn't real, after all. Had he imagined it to keep from falling into a pit of despair?

"Scott, it's Breanna. Are you out there?"

Bree was here? But why was she with the man who tried to kidnap him from the hospital?

"Scott, it's Officer McBride from yesterday. I'm with your friend, Breanna. We're here to help. Where are you, buddy?"

"Breanna," Scott said with as much force as he could manage. "Over here."

He tried sitting up, but his body felt as though someone had pumped lead into his veins. He could hardly move. "Breanna."

A light flashed above him, and then pinned him with its powerful beam.

"Scott." She came into view, a frown of worry creasing her forehead.

"You're here," he said.

"I'm here." She smiled, a smile that made everything right.

Relief drifted over him like a thick blanket on a cold winter's night. He studied her green eyes, and a sense of calm washed over him.

"Are you okay?" she said. "Did he hurt you?"

"I...I'm tired."

"It's okay. We can talk later."

She stroked his hair. He leaned into her touch knowing he was safe as long as she was near.

Bree spent the next day sticking close to Scott, more like hovering, until he was discharged in the afternoon. She didn't trust the hospital to keep him safe from his attackers after the incident last night. The men who were after Scott were terribly bold to impersonate a deputy and attempt to kidnap him from the hospital.

Bree had told Chief Washburn she thought she'd heard Dr. Vann's voice in the stairwell, but it turned out the doctor was off duty so it couldn't have been him.

Rather than ruminate about what had nearly happened, she focused on the positive—Scott was okay. She held his hand and comforted him when he thrashed in his sleep, and hoped that he'd wake up and remember something that could help him defend himself against these men.

When he finally awoke, he didn't remember much more than he had when they'd first brought him in. Thankfully someone had recognized him from photos the local police were circulating and identified him as Scott James, a guest at Echo Mountain Resort. Bree heard from Ryan that Chief Washburn was checking with Chicago and Detroit police departments to confirm Scott's identity.

Dr. Vann wasn't convinced Scott should be discharged considering he'd been drugged last night, but Scott wanted out of the hospital and Bree couldn't blame him.

Chief Washburn sent Officer Carrington to escort them to the resort, probably at the urging of her uncle Chuck, who still worried that she was developing an unhealthy attachment to Scott.

The hospital volunteer pushed Scott to the exit door in a wheelchair and he stood, tentatively. Bree gripped his arm for support.

"Thanks," he said, gazing down into her eyes.

It was that look, a look of deep appreciation tinted with fear that kept her close. He shifted into the front seat of the SUV and she shut the door. Fiona started barking in the back, so Bree tapped on the window. "Stop."

Fiona sat and stopped barking. What did Bree expect? There was a new person sitting in the front seat and Fiona hadn't been officially introduced. How dare Bree allow a stranger into her car.

Into her heart.

She buried that unwelcome thought and got behind the wheel. "Sorry about the dog. She's protective."

"A good thing," he said. "You're lucky to have her."

Bree pulled away from the hospital and spotted Officer Carrington in the rear view mirror following close behind.

"Breanna?"

"Yes?"

"I have no idea what's going to happen next, but I wanted to make sure I said thank you for everything you've done."

"You're welcome."

"I'd probably be dead if it weren't for you."

She knew firsthand that focusing on the darkness only made things worse so she tried to lighten things a little.

"Right, a good thing I'd been hanging out in a tree, trying to outwit the K9 dogs."

"Is that why you were there?"

"Yep, it was the final test to approve them for duty."

"And you were in the tree because hikers climb trees after they're wounded and immobilized?" The corner of his mouth curled.

Good, he had a sense of humor. That would get him through the tough road ahead, both the physical recovery and the violence that seemed to be hounding him.

"A hiker could fall and get stuck in a tree, or a paraglider could miscalculate his landing, or—"

"I get it, I get it," he said with a smile.

Her heart skipped. His genuine smile was the first pleasant interaction they'd had. Everything else up to this point had been tainted with worry or panic on his part, and determined protection on hers.

"What?" he said, studying her.

"What, what?"

"You look, I don't know, pleased."

"You smiled." She glanced back at the road. "It's nice to see you smile."

A few seconds of silence passed. Breanna couldn't help but wonder who this man really was and if he had family, or a wife. It didn't matter. She would offer assistance until his family showed up to care for him.

"Can I ask you something?" he said.

"Of course."

"Why are you doing this?"

"Driving you to the resort? That's where you're staying. Don't you remember?"

"I meant, why are you helping me?"

"Because it's the right thing to do."

"Why do I sense there's more to it?"

Interesting that he could read her so easily when she'd been told by plenty of people that she often came off as aloof and detached. Well, ever since her time under Thomas's rule, anyway. That's when she'd learned to hide her true feelings so he wouldn't be able to use them against her.

"I'm sorry," Scott said.

She snapped her attention to him briefly, then refocused on the road. "Excuse me?"

"Your expression turned terribly sad. I sense it's my fault."

"It's not you. I was remembering something."

"Bad, huh?"

"An old boyfriend and how he controlled me."

"You're kidding." He chuckled.

"You're laughing at me?" she said, her tone more hurt than angry.

"Wait, no, I'm sorry, it's just, the way you ordered hospital staff around, the demanding tone you took with sheriff's deputies—"

"That was one deputy and he's my cousin."

"Trust me, from where I'm sitting, you're definitely in control."

"Thanks, I'll take that as a compliment."

"Good. I would not want to get on your bad side. You know karate." He winked.

"You really are remembering things."

"I remember stuff since the accident, but not what happened leading up to it." He glanced out the passenger window. "That would be the most helpful right now."

"It'll come back to you."

"I hope it's not too late."

"Too late for what?"

He glanced at her and frowned. "I'm not sure."

She exited the expressway and headed for the resort.

"After you drop me at the resort, we can't see each other again," he announced.

"Whoa, I've heard brain injuries can cause rude behavior, but that was a little over the top."

"I'm trying to protect you."

"First things first. I'll help you get settled in your room, then we can argue about breaking up," she joked.

"You seem awfully cavalier about this."

"I don't mean to come off that way, but focusing on the negative stuff only stresses us out more."

She parked in the back lot and pointed at her two-bedroom cottage in the distance. "That's my place, if you ever need anything." She opened her door. "Come on, Fiona and I will get you settled."

She got out of the car and shook off the odd, painful sting she'd felt when he said he never wanted to see her again. He was only considering her well-being.

Officer Carrington pulled his cruiser into the spot next to Bree's.

She opened the hatch and let Fiona out of the back of the truck. The dog immediately ran up to Scott to check him out. Although most golden retrievers were happy pups, Fiona tended to be wary of people. Yet she wasn't wary of Scott. Fiona did her hip wiggle dance, wagging her tail enthusiastically. Scott reached down and stroked her head. Fiona posed in a perfect dog sit and looked up at him.

"She's a sweetheart," he said.

"She has her moments." Bree smiled down at her puppy. She still considered the two-year-old dog a pup since she could play for hours and never get tired. A good trait for a rescue dog.

Officer Carrington joined them as they headed for the building. "I'd like to go in first," he said.

"Whatever you think is best." Bree motioned him ahead. "He's in room one twelve, on the right."

They went into the building, Fiona trotting between Bree and Scott like a proud pup. Scott seemed to be walking steadily, not like before at the hospital.

"You're feeling better?" she asked.

"Head still hurts, but my vision's pretty clear and I don't feel like the floor is shifting on me."

"That's a good sign," she encouraged.

They got to his room and she handed the key card to the officer.

"Please wait out here," he said.

"Of course." She leaned against the wall and sighed.

Scott studied her. "You have to be beat."

"What makes you say that?"

"Every time I opened my eyes you were there, so I'm assuming you haven't gotten much sleep in the past two days."

"I can function on very few hours of sleep."

"Then why haven't you finished cleaning

up around the tennis court?" Aiden said, walking up to them.

Fiona started to rush Aiden, but Bree gave her the command to stay.

"Scott, this is my brother Aiden."

"The manager of the resort," Scott said, shaking Aiden's hand.

"One and the same. And being manager, I can decide if a guest has overstayed his welcome."

"Aiden," she said in a scolding tone.

He ignored her and leveled Scott with a threatening squint of his eyes. "After they find your ID and wallet, I'll expect you to be checking out."

Bree grabbed his arm and pulled him away from Scott. "What's the matter with you?"

"It's dangerous for him to be here."

"It was dangerous when those men were after Billie, but you let her stay here."

"That's different. She's family."

"It's okay," Scott said. "He's right. I'll leave as soon as I can."

The door to his room opened and Officer Carrington motioned them inside. "All clear."

Scott went into the room and Bree followed.

"Bree, where are you going?" Aiden said.

"Someone in our family should be hospi-table. Fiona, come."

The golden rushed to her master's side, they went into the room and shut the door on her brother.

She bit back her embarrassment at Aiden's behavior and took in her surroundings. It was a mini-suite complete with kitchenette, living room and separate bedroom. These rooms were designed for extended stays.

"I've been ordered to keep you under sur-veillance, Scott," Officer Carrington said. "If nothing else, the sight of the cruiser in the lot and me outside your door might deter the assailants from returning."

"Great, thanks." As Scott ambled to the sliding glass door he touched a suit jacket stretched across a chair as if it looked for-eign to him.

"I'm going to patrol the grounds out back." With a nod, Officer Carrington left.

Bree didn't like the odd look creasing Scott's features but before she could question him her phone vibrated with a call. She glanced at the screen. "It's my mom."

"Your brother is right," he said, staring out across the grounds. "You should go."

She went to him and touched his shoulder. "I'm not going anywhere until I know you're okay, but I need to take this call."

He nodded, not looking at her.

"Hey, Mom." She went to the kitchenette.

"Honey, I got a call from Aiden."

"Wow, that was fast." Bree glanced inside the fridge. It had a carton of orange juice and a few to-go containers.

"He's worried about you. We're all worried."

"Thank you for that. I'm blessed to have such a loving family."

She glanced at Scott, who disappeared into the bedroom.

"Don't get me wrong," Mom said. "You're doing a wonderful thing, Breanna. But your brother and I are concerned that Scott's problems will become your problems, that the danger will spill onto you."

"Scott's been assigned 24-hour police protection so he's safe. Also, since we're at the resort we'll get Harvey to help keep an eye on things."

"Yes, well that makes me feel a little better. Harvey would never let anything happen to you."

True enough. Bree shared a special bond with Harvey, the resort's security manager. She considered him more of a father figure than a coworker.

"Everything will be fine, Mom."

"You sound so sure of yourself."

"You're going to have to trust that I wouldn't put myself in unnecessary danger."

"I...I'd like to believe that."

Bree could hear the question in Mom's voice, probably because she was remembering all the months when Bree claimed to be fine, when in fact she was not.

"Don't worry," Bree said.

Hoping to assuage Scott's worry about Bree's safety as well as her mom's, she wandered toward the bedroom and said, "I'm perfectly safe."

Bree stopped short in the doorway.

Scott sat on the bed gripping a pistol in his hand.

FIVE

"I'll call you later, Mom." Bree pocketed her phone and took a deep breath to calm her frantic pulse.

"Scott?"

"I found this on the nightstand." He glanced at her with confusion in his eyes. "Why do I have a gun?"

"I'm sure you had a good reason."

"I'm not a cop anymore, I know that much."

"Why do you say that?"

"A cop would never carry a .50 caliber cannon like this. It's overkill."

He placed the gun on the bed beside him. "Call Officer Carrington, or your cousin, or the police chief. I need to be arrested."

"For owning a firearm?" she said, walking over and sitting next to him on the bed. "Lots of people own guns."

"Don't try to make this okay, Breanna." He stood and paced to the window. "It's not okay."

A few seconds of silence passed between them. She wanted to help, but wasn't sure how. Telling him everything was going to be okay didn't seem to comfort him.

"Call the sheriff's office and have them take me in to be fingerprinted."

"Don't you think you should rest first?"

He turned to her, his eyes now dark with anger. "Call them, or I'll call 9-1-1."

She ignored his threatening expression because she sensed the anger was directed at himself. "I'll get Officer Carrington."

She plucked the gun from the bed by its grip, walked it into the main living area and placed it on the breakfast bar. Although her words were meant to calm them both, she realized this changed things. If he didn't have a permit for the gun, which he probably didn't since his wallet had been stolen, then could he be arrested for illegal possession of a firearm?

Grabbing the wall phone, she called the security office to enlist Harvey's help.

"Security," he answered.

"Harvey, it's Breanna."

"Hey, Bree, how's our amnesiac guest?"

"Word travels fast. Harvey, I have a situation and need your help."

"Name it."

"I have to track down the police officer assigned to Scott. He's on the grounds somewhere and I need him to come to Scott's room."

"I'll find him. Everything okay?"

"Sure." She glanced into the bedroom. Scott flopped down on his back, his good arm draped over his face.

"Let me know when you find him, and maybe you'll want to come by, too."

"I'm on it."

She ended the call and went into the bedroom to sit beside Scott. He must have felt the bed shift because he opened his eyes and looked at her. "You need to go."

"Scott—"

"Now! Get out of here!" He got up, marched into the bathroom and slammed the door.

Scott stared into the mirror at his harried expression: his cheeks red with anger, his eyes wild with fear. If the woman had any sense at all she'd be gone when he opened the bathroom door because the way he looked right now scared even Scott.

If only he could escape himself, he mused, flipping on the tap. He splashed his face with cold water. This self-pity was starting to wear on him. He wasn't that guy, the kind of man who let things happen to him without trying to defend himself. Yet with only part of his brain functioning, he felt more than a little frustrated.

And lost.

Except when he was looking into Bree's beautiful green eyes.

"That's a side effect the brain trauma," he told himself.

It had to be. Women were not something you relied on for strength, at least that had been Scott's experience. He practically raised both his mom and little sister after Dad had left, and as far as romantic relationships... He pinched his eyes shut, trying to remember something, someone.

But only a high school girlfriend who broke it off when she went to college, and a few fleeting trysts filtered into his thoughts.

Yet he thought there had been a more serious relationship.

His head started to pound. "What difference does it make?" he muttered. Once the cops came and retrieved his gun, he'd be arrested for sure.

He felt himself being sucked into the self-pitying vortex again and fought it. There was more at stake than Scott's personal situation, a lot more.

The doctors had warned him that a head injury could cause emotional highs and lows, anger issues and even symptoms of depression. Whatever. He didn't have the luxury of suffering from such ailments.

It was time to pull himself out of this funk and face his situation head-on, without the help of his beautiful and caring crutch named Breanna.

He finger-combed his hair back off his face and took a steadying breath. Somehow he needed to get his memory back. That had to be his primary focus.

He opened the door to an empty bedroom. Good, she left as he'd requested. Still, he went into the main living area to be sure.

An older man in his mid-sixties glanced up

from analyzing the gun on the breakfast bar. "I'm Harvey, the resort security manager. Officer Carrington should be here shortly." Harvey walked over and shook Scott's hand. "Sorry to hear about your situation. Bree told me you don't remember anything leading up to the assault."

"Bree, is she…?"

"Gone. Got a SAR call."

"SAR?" Scott asked.

"Search and rescue. A kid went missing on a field trip into the mountains. They called in the K9 team to assist, hoping the dogs could track her quickly. So—" Harvey sat at the breakfast bar "—want to tell me about this gun?"

"Wish I could."

"Don't remember much, huh?" Harvey pressed.

"No, sir, although, I was a cop. I remember that much."

"Well, we have that in common."

"You were on the job?" Scott shifted onto a bar stool.

"Yep, Seattle P.D. This is my official retirement." Someone knocked on the door.

"That'll be Officer Carrington." Harvey went to let him in.

"Where is he?" an angry voice said.

"Aiden, cool your jets."

Bree's brother stormed around the corner and came at Scott. "You brought a gun into my resort?"

Aiden grabbed Scott by the arm, ripped him off the bar stool and shoved him against the wall. Pain reverberated down Scott's arm from the gunshot wound to his fingertips.

"My sister was in this room, with a gun?" Aiden slugged him in the jaw and stars crossed Scott's vision.

"That's enough!" Harvey pulled Aiden off of Scott.

Scott swiped at his lip with the back of his hand and eyed his attacker. "I'm sorry."

That only infuriated him more. Aiden broke free of Harvey and pinned Scott against the wall yet again. This time he hesitated before striking.

"Do it," Scott said. "Just do it."

Scott deserved the beating and then some. He'd failed so many people in his life, and was about to fail a bunch more.

Aiden glared, his jaw twitching with his

struggle for self-control. Instead of hitting him, he let go with a jerk that banged Scott's head against the wall.

Stars fluttered across Scott's vision again and his legs buckled.

"Whoa, whoa," Harvey said, gripping Scott's arm and guiding him to the couch.

Nausea rolled through Scott's stomach as the room spun.

He must have passed out because the next thing he heard was a rather intense interrogation of Bree's brother, Aiden.

"How hard did you hit him?"

Scott cracked open his eyes. Officer Carrington was firing off the questions.

"Not hard, I didn't hit him that hard. At least I didn't mean to."

"But you did, and now we've got two armed assailants running around Echo Mountain, a questionable firearm and the only one who could shed light on this case is out cold because of you. Give me your hands." Officer Carrington ripped the cuffs off his belt.

This was wrong. Scott understood Aiden's motivation and didn't blame him for being furious. Scott had put Bree in danger by letting her into his room, into his life.

Aiden slowly offered his wrists to the officer.

"No," Scott croaked, sitting up and gripping his head. It ached worse than before. "It's not his fault."

"He admitted to assaulting you," Officer Carrington said.

Squinting, Scott glanced at the officer. "A misunderstanding. I'm not pressing charges."

Aiden cocked his head as if trying to figure out Scott's angle. But there was none. Scott wouldn't be responsible for Bree's brother being charged and taken into custody. She'd never forgive him, and for some reason her opinion of Scott meant a lot right now.

Someone knocked at the door and Harvey opened it. "Chief," he said in greeting.

Chief Washburn marched into the room. "What's going on?" he asked, glancing from Officer Carrington to Aiden, to Scott.

"Supposedly a misunderstanding," Officer Carrington said. "This is what I called about." He handed an evidence bag to the chief with the gun tucked inside.

"A .50 caliber Desert Eagle? Is it registered?" the chief asked.

"I have no idea." Scott massaged his temples. "If I carried registration it would have been in my wallet." Scott glanced up. The chief and Officer Carrington hovered over him, wanting answers. Scott had none.

He glanced at Aiden who sat in a chair studying the floor.

"I would have done the same thing," Scott blurted out.

Aiden glanced at him.

"That's your job as a big brother. I get it. I've been there."

"Focus on the gun, Scott," the chief said.

Scott redirected his attention to the chief. "Sir, if I knew anything I'd tell you."

The chief's phone beeped. He glanced at it and shook his head. "As long as you're being honest," the chief started, then pinned Scott with a serious frown. "You said you were a cop?"

"Yes."

"Then how about telling us why the name

Scott James doesn't come up in any law enforcement databases?"

Bree and Fiona headed into the national park, teamed with Will Rankin. Will would focus on the map while Bree watched Fiona, looking for tell signs. Grace and her lab, Dodger, were accompanied by Griffin Swift, and three other SAR members followed along as well in case the missing child needed to be carried out on a litter. Bree had strapped on her mission-ready pack and was at the trailhead in a matter of minutes.

As they hiked toward the last spot the child was seen, Bree inhaled the crisp mountain air, glad she'd noticed the text on her phone when she had. It gave her something to do, something productive and helpful after being ordered to leave by Scott.

She suspected he pushed her away because he feared for her safety, which only made her respect him more. She knew how strongly he relied on her, so pushing her away must have been extremely difficult.

"So how is he?" Grace said over her shoulder.

"Who?"

"The mysterious Scott? That's who you were thinking about, right?"

"That obvious, huh?"

"Pretty obvious."

Grace was a lovely fortysomething woman with auburn hair, who acted like an older sibling A non-meddling older sibling.

"Scott's better, I guess."

"Must be scary, not remembering anything."

"It puts him in a very vulnerable position," Bree said.

"I can imagine." Grace pulled out her topographical map encased in plastic and reviewed the area. "Should be right up here."

"The rest of the kids came down already?"

"Yes, sheriff's office didn't want to risk more kids wandering off to find their friend so they ordered them to come back down. Here it is." Grace hesitated and glanced back at her team. "Heather was last seen forty-five minutes ago in this general area. Ready?" Grace offered the article of clothing with Heather's scent to each of the dogs.

The three K9 handlers split up, heading into the thick brush of blackberries, devil's club and rotting logs. Bree was glad to have

Will as her partner. He had both field EMT experience and little girl experience, since he had two girls of his own.

Fiona was unusually excited today, perhaps because she didn't get her twice-daily walks for the past few days and had extra energy.

"That's it, Fiona. Good girl," Bree encouraged.

"Heather!" Grace called out, although they all suspected the little girl must be unconscious or she would have answered to her teachers and friends calling out her name earlier.

Bree glanced at the sky. They had plenty of daylight to work with, which was good.

"At least it's decent weather," Will commented. "On my last mission it poured nonstop for five hours."

"Yikes, which one was that?"

"The hiker that got separated from his buddies in Crystal Pass."

"Oh, right. That was a nasty day to be out."

"Bet you're sorry you missed it."

"Very funny. Would have been there, but had a family thing."

"Well, my girls weren't too happy with me when I went out on the call. I said I'd avoid SAR missions for the next month."

"Yet here you are."

"They're with their grandparents."

"Why do you do this, anyway?" she asked. "I mean you're so busy with work and your girls."

"I like to help, you know, find people."

Yes, she understood completely. It felt good to focus on helping someone else rather than ruminating about your own miseries and losses. Will had suffered his share of loss. His wife died of cancer, leaving him to be a single parent.

And Bree? Adopting Fiona and joining SAR when she moved back to town kept her busy and focused on helping others instead of wallowing in her own shame.

"It's certainly a good feeling to be proactive and help people," she offered.

They'd been searching for a good half hour when Fiona started pulling hard on the leash and stuck her nose to the ground.

"What is it, Fi?" Bree said.

A splash of pink stuck out from the dark green brush up ahead. Bree stomped over wild blackberry bushes in an effort to get to Heather.

Please, God, let her be okay.

Fiona rushed to the little girl, sniffing and nudging. "Okay, girl, okay. Grace, we've located Heather, over," Bree said into her radio.

"Coordinates?"

Will rattled them off and kneeled beside Heather to examine the little girl. She was curled up in a ball, but he was able to slide her mitten off to take her pulse.

"It's strong," he said. "Maybe she hit her head."

Fiona went in for a kiss on Heather's cheek. "Fi, no." Bree pulled her back.

"Heather, honey? Can you hear me?" Will said.

She whimpered. Will and Bree shared a look.

"Can you open your eyes?" Will said.

She shook her head no.

"Why not?"

"I'm scared," she moaned.

"Are you hurt?" Will asked.

She shook her head again.

Bree nodded at Will, then at Fiona.

"Good idea," Will said softly.

"Heather, honey, I need your help," Bree said. "My dog, Fiona, is scared, too. You know why?"

Heather nodded she didn't.

"Because she's worried about you. Can you open your eyes and tell Fiona you're okay?"

The little girl blinked a few times, and opened her eyes. Bree relaxed the leash and Fiona went in for a sniff. Heather giggled and reached out to pet Fiona.

"Thank you so much," Bree said. "You ready to go home?"

"Can Fiona come with me?"

Bree smiled. "No, honey, she's got to stay at my place and be ready to find more missing kids like you. But I'll tell you what, she'll walk you down to the trail where your mom and dad are waiting."

"Heather, before you get up, are you sure you didn't fall and hurt yourself?" Will asked.

Heather offered her hand, scratched from a thorny bush.

"How about I clean that out and wrap it?" Will said.

"Will it hurt?"

"Not too much."

"Here." Bree led Fiona to the other side of the little girl. "You can pet Fiona while Will fixes your cut, okay?"

"Okay."

Bree commanded Fiona to lie beside the little girl, and Heather reached out to stroke Fi's head. Bree pressed the button on her radio. "The victim doesn't seem to have any serious injuries, over," she said. "We'll meet you where we split up, over."

"Roger," Grace said.

Fiona crawled closer to Heather and sniffed her cheek. Heather giggled. The golden knew exactly how to distract her from Will's first-aid efforts.

In a few short minutes, he was finished. "Okay, let's get you up," Will said. He put his hands under her armpits and lifted her with ease. Bree suspected he'd done this many times with his girls. "How does that feel? Legs working okay?"

"Yes," she said, not taking her eyes off Fiona, who also stood.

"Great, then let's get you home," Will said. "It's kind of messy out here. Do you think you can walk?"

"Can Fiona carry me?" she said.

"She wishes she could," Bree said. "Here," she handed Heather the leash, and picked her up.

"You sure?" Will asked Bree.

"I'm good." With the little girl in her arms, and both of them holding Fiona's leash, they headed back to the trail.

It had been an emotional afternoon to say the least. She pulled into the driveway of her bungalow and put Fiona into the fenced yard. Harvey jogged up to her.

"Hey there," she said.

"Got word you found her," Harvey said, raising his hand.

She slapped him a high five. "Fiona found her, I just happened to be tagging along."

"You're too modest."

"How's Scott?" she said.

"Scott, he, uh…" Harvey glanced down.

Her blood pressure spiked. "What? He's okay, right?"

"He's okay, but they took him in for questioning."

"Because of the gun?"

"And he's been lying."

"Lying about what?"

"They couldn't find any record of a cop named Scott James."

"I'm sure there's an explanation."

"Probably not a good one."

"Where'd they take him?"

"Bree, leave it alone."

"Wish I could." She pulled open the driver's door and got behind the wheel. "Where?" she said.

"Chief Washburn took him to the station."

"Thanks."

Harvey blocked her from shutting the door. "Be careful."

"If you're worried about Scott, don't be. He'd never hurt me." She pulled the door shut and backed out of the driveway. Fiona was fine outside, and if it started to rain she had the doggie door that gave her access to the kitchen.

As Bree raced into town, she checked the speedometer. She didn't want to get delayed because of a speeding ticket. No, she needed to get to the police station and…and…

What? What was she doing, exactly? One thing for sure, she wasn't thinking straight. She'd told Harvey that Scott would never hurt her. Was she delusional? She didn't know Scott that well. How could she make such a bold statement?

His eyes.

There was something about the look in his eyes that touched her core, reminding her what it felt like to be scared and alone. She'd promised herself she'd never feel that way again, and she surely wouldn't stand by and watch another person be brutalized and not try to help.

Or maybe she was losing her mind.

The emotional afternoon had taken its toll: worrying about a lost girl, praying for her safety, finding her, and at first thinking she was...dead.

And then Bree had carried her out of the brush, emotions tangling up even more at the feel of a little girl depending on Bree, needing her so badly. Would Bree ever have a child of her own? Hold a child of her own?

Wow, talk about an emotional volcano. Bree was all over the place. Maybe so, but she knew one thing: Scott was being interrogated and had no one in his corner.

That is, until she got there.

Ten minutes later she pulled onto Main

Street and looked for a spot in the lot, but it was full. She parked across the street and glanced out her window. The chief was escorting Scott out of the building. Now where were they taking him? She flung open her car door.

"Scott!" she called.

She thought he spotted her, but looked quickly away as the chief led him to a squad car. She glanced both ways to safely cross the street.

"Hey!" she called out again and took a step.

The squeal of tires made her glance over her shoulder. A black car sped up and stopped abruptly in front of her. The passenger door opened and a man wearing dark sunglasses and a low-hung baseball cap said, "Get in."

Was he nuts?

"No, thank you," Bree said.

"I said—" he placed a gun on the driver's seat in a not-so-subtle threat "—get in."

SIX

"Something's wrong," Scott said to the chief, eyeing Bree as she spoke with the driver in the black sedan.

There was something about her expression that made Scott head in her direction.

"Where are you going?" Chief Washburn said.

"She's in trouble."

Scott took off, not considering what he'd do once he got to the car, or how embarrassed he'd be if his instincts, like his brain, were off-line.

He wanted to call out, let her know he was coming to help, but he couldn't even speak, panic strangling his vocal cords.

"Scott!" Chief Washburn called.

Scott hoped the chief followed him. At least the guy had a firearm. Scott had nothing but a sincere desire to protect Bree.

Dodging into the street, Scott was hyper-focused on the lovely but terrified blonde who stepped away from the car with a horrified look on her face.

"Bree!" Scott called.

A car horn screamed.

Brakes squealed.

Scott glanced to his left in time to see a compact car skidding toward him. The driver spun the wheel at the last second and the small car slid past Scott and slammed into a parked car. Scott turned back to the dark sedan just as the driver peeled away, burning rubber on the street.

Without hesitation, he went to Bree and placed gentle hands on her shoulders. "Are you okay?"

She nodded, but he could tell she was traumatized.

"What was that about?" Chief Washburn said, rushing up to Scott and Bree. He led them between parked cars to the sidewalk as he spoke into his radio. "We need an officer on Main Street. There's been an accident." He redirected his attention to Bree. "You okay?"

"The man in that black car threatened me."

"Threatened you how?"

"He told me to get in, then he flashed a gun."

"Did you recognize him?" the chief asked.

"No, sir."

Scott automatically pulled Bree against his chest into a gentle hug. "It's okay, he's gone."

"Did either of you get a plate number?" the chief asked.

Bree shook her head.

"I think the first three letters were AGE," Scott offered.

The chief took a few steps away and spoke into his shoulder radio again, telling officers to be on the look-out for the black sedan. Scott stroked Bree's soft hair in a calming gesture. "You're okay."

She leaned back and looked up into his eyes. "Thanks to you."

"I wouldn't go that far."

"I would. If you hadn't drawn attention to him I might have been in his car headed to who knows where."

"But you didn't get in his car. Smart girl."

"We'll keep an eye out for him," the chief said.

Bree broke the hug, but Scott kept a protective arm around her shoulder.

"Scott saved my life, Chief."

The chief nodded at Bree. "How about you come into the station and give an official statement about what happened?"

"Sure."

"Head back inside while I check on the driver over there."

"Tell her I'm sorry for running in front of her," Scott said.

With a nod, the chief jogged across the street and spoke with the teenager who stared at her crushed front bumper, with her hands framing her face.

"Come on, let's go," Scott said.

Bree stepped away from Scott's protective hold and he wondered if she thought it inappropriate, or if she was worried about town gossips. There were plenty of gawkers out here getting a look at the fender bender. He respected her need for space and didn't push it.

As they crossed the street and headed into the P.D. parking lot, he felt her hand slide into his. He gave her fingers a squeeze, and only then did he notice they were trembling.

He glanced at her, but you'd never guess by her expression that she was rattled. With a firm clench of her jaw and pleasant expression, she walked across the lot toward the police department. No one would suspect she was probably on the verge of bursting into tears.

And if she did, he'd be right there to comfort her.

They stepped into the police station where a twenty-something secretary was focused on paperwork.

"Hi, Audrey," Bree said.

Audrey the secretary glanced up. "Breanna, what are you doing here?"

"There was an accident. I need to give a statement. The chief's outside...." Bree's voice trailed off.

The magnitude of her situation was about to hit her square in the chest.

"Is there a place we can wait privately for the chief?" Scott said.

Audrey narrowed her eyes at him. She didn't like the fact he was here with Bree, probably because Scott had just been questioned by the chief about his real identity.

"He saved my life, Audrey," Bree said. "I really need to sit down."

Audrey snapped her attention to Bree. "Of course, follow me."

Scott and Bree followed Audrey down the hall into a conference room and sat on one side of the table, next to each other.

"Do you want me to call—"

"No," Bree interrupted her. "No need to call anyone. I'll be fine."

With one last narrowing of her eyes at Scott, Audrey went back to her post out front.

"How did it go with the chief?" Bree said.

"We don't have to talk about that now." He took one of her hands in his own and stroked it gently. "You're still shaken up."

"Thanks, but it will distract me from what just happened," she said.

"Ah, so you're using my ill fortunes to distract you from your own? I didn't think you were that kind of girl," he teased.

"Ha ha." She cracked a slight smile. "So, what did I miss when I was on the mission?"

"First tell me how the mission went."

"Good. We found the little girl. She's okay," she said with a faraway look in her eye.

"Breanna?" he prompted.

"That look on her face of complete and utter fear...." She hesitated. "It stays with you for a while."

"But you found her. Everything's okay?"

"Well, everything was okay until Harvey told me you were brought in for questioning. Did they advise you of your rights? Do you need a lawyer? I have a friend who's an attorney. I could call—"

"I wasn't arrested. They thought finger-printing me might be helpful, so they did. I hope..." He glanced at their hands.

"What?"

"I hope they don't find out I'm a murder suspect or drug dealer or something."

"Hey, don't talk like that. You said you were a cop."

He shrugged. "Even cops go bad."

"Scott, look at me."

He glanced up. She shot him that peaceful, tender smile that seemed to calm every frantic thought in his mind.

"You are not a criminal," she said with conviction.

"Thanks for the vote of confidence, but I can't be so sure. I mean, I had a .50 caliber gun in my room." He shook his head, frustrated. "At least once they run the serial number it might answer some questions."

"We're also sending it to ballistics," Chief Washburn said, coming into the room.

"Ballistics? Why?" Bree said.

"So they'll be able to tell if it was used in any other crimes," Scott explained.

"Oh." Bree frowned.

"Let's focus on what happened just now," the chief said, pulling out a chair and joining them at the table. "The driver of the black sedan threatened you with a gun, Breanna?"

"Yes, sir."

"Did he indicate what he wanted?"

"He ordered me to get in the car."

"Did he give a reason?" The chief jotted something down.

"No, sir."

"I need you to tell me exactly what he said."

"He said 'get in.' When I didn't…" She glanced at Scott and then down at the floor.

"What?" Scott said.

She sighed. "He said if I wanted to know what my boyfriend was into that I'd get in the car and he'd show me."

"Show you what?" the chief asked.

"I have no idea."

Scott stood and paced to the window overlooking the parking lot. "So I *am* into something illegal."

"Wait, you're going to believe the word of a man who tried to kidnap me at gunpoint?" Bree challenged.

"There's no reason to think he's lying," Scott said.

"Actually, there is," the chief said.

Scott turned around.

"I got the report that Scott James has no priors or known criminal activity."

"See," Bree said.

"Maybe I just haven't been caught."

Bree couldn't stand the look in Scott's eyes, one of desperation and shame. But he had nothing to be ashamed of, at least nothing they knew about yet.

She gave him a ride back to the resort and an officer followed close behind. Even though Bree felt confident Scott wasn't the bad guy here, others in the community, especially law enforcement, weren't so sure.

The chief must have notified Aiden about the developments, because he was waiting for them when she pulled into her parking spot.

"He doesn't look happy," Scott said.

She turned off the car and Aiden opened her door. "We need to talk."

"Okay. I was going to walk Scott to his room."

"That's why Officer Carrington is here, right?" Aiden said.

"I was going to check the dressing on his shoulder wound."

"What, are you his private nurse now?"

"Why are you being so rude? Scott saved my life."

Aiden glared at Scott. "You wouldn't have needed the save if he'd never come to Echo Mountain."

"Get out of my way." Bree brushed past him. "Come on, Scott."

When he didn't follow, she turned around. Scott slowly approached her. "I don't want to be the reason that you and your brother fight," he said. "I appreciate you wanting to help, but you've done more than enough for me." With a grateful smile, he headed for the resort. The officer followed him.

It sounded as though he was dismissing

her from her duties. But this didn't feel like a duty. It felt right and natural to be helping him.

"He'll be fine," Aiden said.

She spun around. "Why do you hate him so much? You don't even know him."

"And you do?" he snapped.

After the emotional day she'd had, she didn't need her big brother criticizing her. She marched toward her cottage.

"Wait, Bree."

She kept walking, fuming about everything that had happened in the past forty-eight hours, from her brother's rudeness toward a wounded man in need, to a stranger threatening her with a gun.

It seemed strange that Scott's enemies would hang around town considering law enforcement was on the lookout for suspicious characters. Whatever they were into must be incredibly important.

Not her problem or concern. Her only concern was doing right by Scott.

As she approached her home, Fiona rushed the fence and barked her greeting. "Hey, girl," Bree said.

"Bree, stop ignoring me," Aiden said, stepping up beside her.

She opened the gate and let Fiona out to give her a hug. "You could learn some manners from my dog," she said to her brother.

She led Fiona up to the front porch and sat in the rocker. "You want to talk to me? Talk," she said.

"Stop being so angry." He leaned against the porch railing.

"Wow, you're even telling me how I should feel? That doesn't sound like Thomas," she said in a sarcastic tone.

She knew the words were harsh, but couldn't stop them from tumbling out of her mouth. Essentially it was the truth. Aiden was acting like an overbearing, domineering male.

Aiden crossed his arms over his chest. "I guess I deserved that." He glanced her. "But try to understand where I'm coming from. You're obsessed with a guy who's obviously into something dangerous."

"He's not into something dangerous. Danger is finding him."

"It's the same thing."

"No, it isn't."

"I don't want to argue semantics."

"You started it."

"And now we're twelve again," he muttered.

Bree continued to stroke an enthusiastic Fiona, but didn't respond to Aiden. What could she say? He was right. They were fighting like kids.

"Let me try again," he said. "All my life it's been my job to protect my baby sisters. I thought I did an okay job, then you moved to Seattle and I couldn't protect you. And now…this situation with Scott feels like the same thing."

"But it's totally different. Thomas was a manipulating bully who'd convinced me I was a failure without him. Scott is a gentle, wounded soul who needs our help. Have you even talked to him?"

"It doesn't matter." He shook his head. "I failed you with Thomas and this feels like it's happening all over again." He pushed away from the railing and paced to the top of the steps. "Right here in my own resort."

"Aiden—"

"Try to understand, Bree, okay?" he said, not looking at her.

"Sure." She hesitated. "But could you do me a favor and ease up a little? Get to know Scott before you make assumptions?"

"I'll try." He started down the porch steps. "You going by Mom's tonight?"

"No. Chief Washburn is sending over a forensic artist to meet with me and Scott."

"Text me if you need anything."

"Will do, thanks."

Her big brother headed to the main building looking a bit defeated. A part of her understood his need to protect her and she greatly appreciated it, but another part resented the inference that she couldn't take care of herself. She'd done pretty well. She'd saved Scott from the bad guys in the mountains and today she'd avoided being kidnapped. She had Scott to thank for that. If he hadn't come racing across the street to accost the driver Bree might have been forced into the car.

Scott may think she'd done her duty and didn't need to help him any longer, but she disagreed. She would feed Fiona, whip up her specialty, mac and cheese, and head to Scott's room with dinner. The forensic artist could meet her there and the three of them could work on the sketch.

She glanced across the property at Scott's room. The curtains were drawn. She hoped he was resting. Lord knows if she suffered a gunshot wound and mind-numbing concussion she'd welcome the healing benefits of sleep. Still, he had to eat. She took Fiona inside and got to work on dinner.

Scott awakened with a start. He gasped and sat up in bed, fighting the violent images of a young woman being tossed out of a moving car onto the pavement. He rushed to her side, turned her over.

Bree. It had been Bree's face staring back at him.

He flopped back down in bed. "Only a dream."

But it felt real, his panic strangling his vocal cords, tying his chest in knots and cutting off his ability to breathe or think straight.

A soft knock tapped at the door. Must be the forensic sketch artist, either that or the officer telling Scott he was leaving for the night. They couldn't possibly keep an eye on him 24/7. No department had that kind of budget, especially a small department like Echo Mountain P.D.

The tapping grew insistent. Scott sat up a little too quickly and his head pounded. Time for more aspirin.

"Coming!" he called out.

He stood, surprised that he didn't waver or grow faint. Man, he hated being this weak, this out of it. He padded to the door and looked through the peephole: Breanna smiled back at him. She held a large bag in her arms.

He pressed his forehead against the door. He wished he could ignore her or tell her to leave him alone. It was the best thing for both of them. Well, the best thing for her, anyway. Scott knew that he had a better chance at surviving the next few days with Bree in his life.

"You okay?" her muffled voice called through the door.

He swung it open and forced a smile. "Sure, I wasn't expecting you."

"I tried calling but no one answered."

"I unplugged the phone."

An apologetic expression creased her features. "I didn't wake you, did I?"

"Nope."

"I did wake you and you're being nice. I'm sorry."

"No, I was awake, honest."

"Have you eaten dinner yet?"

"No, I thought about ordering room service."

"Not necessary." She brushed past him into the room. "I made sandwiches, green salad and my famous macaroni and cheese." She placed the bag on the table and started pulling out containers. "It would be nice to have company for a change while I eat. I mean, other than canine company."

He stood there, holding the door open. A part of him wanted to convince her to leave because she was putting her life at risk just by being here.

"This is a high-carb meal so we should both sleep great tonight."

He couldn't take his eyes off her carefree smile. You never would have guessed she'd been threatened a few hours ago.

Because of him.

"Bree—"

"Sir," Officer Carrington said, stepping into the doorway, "you should keep the door closed."

"Right, thanks. You're not staying all night, are you?" he asked the officer.

"No, sir. Someone's relieving me in about twenty minutes."

"Come on, before it gets cold," Bree called from the table.

"Thanks," Scott said to the cop and shut the door.

"The weather's crazy outside," Bree said. "The wind's blowing like a Kansas tornado is about to touch down."

"When did that start?"

"Last hour or so. Would you like ham and Swiss or turkey and cheddar?" She held out two foil-wrapped sandwiches.

"Whichever one you don't want."

"That's not an answer. Come on, pick."

"Turkey cheddar."

"Great. Have a seat."

She set the table with paper plates, napkins and forks, put a sandwich on each plate and peeled the lid off a plastic bowl containing a green salad. "Hope you're okay with vinaigrette dressing."

"That's fine." He sat and clenched his jaw against the pain of his bruised ribs.

"Looks like you need a pain reliever." She dug in her purse and pulled out a bottle of acetaminophen. She set it on the table beside her keys. He noticed her key chain read: *Let Go, Let God.*

"It's a gentle reminder when I get frantic," she said, eyeing him.

Frantic because of the mess he'd dragged her into these past few days.

"Help yourself," she said, like they were old friends enjoying a meal.

But they weren't old friends. They were strangers, and she was an innocent bystander threatened by the violence trailing him.

"You shouldn't be here," he said, rubbing his forehead.

"And where should I be?"

"You know what I mean."

"I think I do. What you were trying to say was, 'thank you, Bree, for bringing me a homemade meal so I didn't have to order room service.' Notice how I said homemade, not home-cooked. The only thing I cooked is this." Eyes widening with anticipation, she pulled the top off the macaroni and cheese.

"That smells amazing," he said.

"Makes you change your mind about wanting me to leave, huh?" She smiled and shoved a serving spoon into the pasta.

"I never said I wanted you to leave, but we both know the danger of you being here."

"What danger? We're locked in this room with a cop standing guard outside that door. Relax and enjoy some carbs with me. Wait until you see what I brought for dessert." She rubbed her hands together like a kid on Christmas morning.

Suddenly the lights went out.

SEVEN

"Scott?" Breanna said.

Scott could feel the fear floating off her body.

"Place your hand on the table between us," he said. He sensed her body shift. He reached out and slid his hand over hers. Their fingers automatically curled into a perfect hold.

"It's okay. I won't let anyone hurt you," he said. How was he going to manage that when he couldn't see anything and didn't have a weapon to defend them?

"It's probably the generator," she said with false confidence.

"Has this happened before?" He stroked the back of her hand with his thumb.

"The power has flickered before but it's never gone totally out."

When she squeezed his hand he knew he had to do something to make her feel safe.

"I'm going to check in with Officer Carrington," he said.

"Don't let go."

"Okay, then why don't *we* check in with him?"

He stood and led her by the hand to the door.

"This is awfully creepy," she whispered.

"Yeah." And if it had anything to do with Scott's situation, he was going to figure out a way to check out of this hotel and stop putting these people in danger.

They stepped up to the door. "I'll open the door but you stay out of sight."

"Okay."

He cracked open the door and peered into a pitch-black hallway.

A beam of a flashlight hit Scott square in the chest. "Stay in your room," Officer Carrington said. "I'll find out what's going on. Lock your door and don't open it to anyone but me."

Scott shut and locked the door. Adrenaline coursed through him. He had to get control of this situation, if nothing else, for Bree's sake.

"Wait," she said, "I'm an idiot."

"I'm sorry?"

"I have a flashlight app on my phone."

She dug into her pocket. The glow from her cell phone illuminated her beautiful face. She pressed the screen a few times and a flashlight beam lit the area around them.

"See, not so scary," she said, directing the light into the room.

Something knocked against the window and she jumped.

"Bathroom," he said. With his arm around her shoulder, he led her into the roomy bathroom and locked the door. "Extra precaution," he said. That made two doors someone would have to get through to get to them.

"What now?" she said.

"We wait for the all-clear from Officer Carrington."

"I hate waiting." She sat on the closed toilet seat, shining her light across the sink area where he'd spread out his toiletries. He felt exposed, as if getting a glimpse of his personal things gave her yet a closer look into his soul.

Scott shifted to the floor, pressing his back against the bathroom door. An assailant would have to get through Scott to hurt Bree. Yet how much damage could Scott do considering his weakened physical condition? That got him thinking.

"Can you swing that light across the sink area again?" he said.

She did and he looked for something, anything to use as a weapon. Not much you could do with shaving cream, toothpaste and deodorant. Then he spotted a blow-dryer. He got up and grabbed it, weighing it in his hand.

"What are you thinking?" she said.

"Not sure yet. Trying to get creative in case we have unexpected company." He sat back down.

She pointed the flashlight at the ceiling to light up the bathroom. Even from here he could see her worried expression.

"It's probably an outage from the storm," he suggested.

"That makes sense. It was wild out there."

"Lots of stuff blowing around?"

"Yep. Resort staff were chasing after patio chairs."

"That's probably what hit our window."

"Wait, why don't I call Aiden and ask him what's going on?" She reached for the phone and hesitated. "Probably a bad idea."

"Why's that?"

"He's got enough on his hands without his little sister pestering him."

"He'll want to know that you're okay," Scott offered.

"I guess." She eyed the phone but didn't make the call.

"Breanna, what's the hesitation?"

"He'll freak when he finds out where I am."

"Understandable. Well, I'm not letting you leave until the lights come on and I know you're safe."

"Wait, I can call Harvey, or at least text him." She grabbed the phone and texted a message, then reactivated the flashlight app and aimed it toward the ceiling. "He's probably crazed because of the outage."

A sudden pounding echoed from the outer door. Bree sat straight.

"They can't get in without a key card," Scott assured, but she didn't look convinced.

The pounding stopped. Bree's green eyes widened with fear. Scott got up and rubbed her shoulder. "It's okay."

Someone pounded on the bathroom door and Bree yelped.

"What's going on in there?" Aiden demanded.

"Aiden?" she said.

"Bree? Open the door!"

Bree made a face at Scott. This was going to be ugly.

Scott reached for the door, but she grabbed his shirtsleeve. "I'd better open it."

She took a deep breath, stood and opened the door. Her brother shined a flashlight in her face.

"Hey, point that someplace else," she protested.

He aimed it at Scott, who put up his hand to block the beam. The intense light started to spike a headache.

"What are you doing here?" Aiden said, glaring at Bree.

"Waiting for the forensic artist," she said. "We were about to eat dinner when the lights went out."

"You were about to eat dinner," Aiden said, his tone flat.

"What's with the power outage?" Bree asked.

"If you were about to eat dinner, then why were you hiding in the bathroom?" Aiden said, ignoring her question.

"Scott thought it was the safest place to be. So, is it the storm?"

Her brother didn't answer for a few seconds. Scott couldn't see Aiden's expression because it would require Scott to look directly into the flashlight, but he could guess the guy was shooting him death ray eyes.

"Yes, we think it's the storm," Aiden said. "Maintenance is out there checking the lines." He lowered the flashlight and glared at Scott. "But if it's something else, if someone intentionally—"

The lights popped on.

"That was quick," Bree said.

"Not quick enough," Aiden countered, motioning them out of the bathroom. "We lost all power, even emergency lights. That doesn't reflect well on the safety of our guests."

Scott understood Aiden's anger toward

him if this hadn't been a weather-related incident. Scott had already made up his mind he was leaving if that were the case.

Aiden's phone rang and he ripped it off his belt. "What have you got, Harvey?"

As Aiden paced the room, Scott's muscles tensed. He remembered Harvey was the resort's security manager, so Scott was intent on watching Aiden's reaction to the call.

"Yep, okay. That's good news." Aiden glanced at Scott, then at Bree. She was busy spooning macaroni and cheese onto plates.

Scott couldn't believe how resilient she was, considering only a minute ago she was trembling in a dark bathroom with a stranger. Well, not exactly a stranger. They'd engaged in more than small talk during the past few days.

She must have caught him looking at her because she narrowed her eyes at him. "What?"

"You amaze me."

She blushed and refocused on her dinner.

"Harvey said lightning hit a transformer and knocked out the power, but he's not sure what happened to the emergency lights since they're on a different system. I've got to go talk to guests, give them coupons for free ice cream cones or something." He sighed and ran his hand through thick, blond hair.

"Thanks for checking up on us," Bree said. "We have plenty of macaroni if you want to stop back later."

"How long are you going to be here?" he said, irritated.

"I don't know, a few hours?" she said, unwrapping her sandwich.

"Bree, you know how I feel about..." Aiden cast a quick glance at Scott.

"It's a bad idea to be around me," Scott said. "I agree."

Aiden glanced at Scott as if trying to figure out if he was being sincere.

"I understand, Aiden," Bree said. "And I'm sorry it upsets you, but I'm helping Scott and nothing either of you say will change my mind. So, let's not have this conversation again because it's starting to give me a headache."

She closed her eyes, put her hands together and silently prayed over her meal. A few seconds later she grabbed her sandwich and took a bite. A happy, peaceful expression eased across her features. She'd surrendered, to God, to her taste buds, to the beauty of being in the moment. She definitely wasn't listening to her brother's protests.

Scott looked at Aiden and said, "Sorry."

"You will be if anything happens to my sister." Aiden stormed out.

Adjusting himself in the chair across from Bree, Scott reached over to open his sandwich and winced.

"Do you want me to—"

"Nope." He clenched his jaw and peeled back the foil from his sandwich.

"Apologies for my brother," she said.

"Not necessary. He's looking out for you."

"And I'm looking out for you."

"Thanks, but I'm a big boy."

"A wounded big boy with limited memory."

He picked up his sandwich and put it back down.

"What's wrong, you don't want the turkey, after all?" she asked.

"Tonight might have been an act of nature, but if it hadn't been and anything had happened to you—"

"Don't focus on the darkness. We're safe.

We've got shelter and food. Let's be grateful for that and enjoy our meal."

Scott struggled to enjoy a peaceful dinner with the image of Bree's terrified expression and the sound of her anxious voice in his mind.

"'I can do all things through Him who gives me strength,'" she said and glanced up. "*Philippians* 4:13. It's one of my favorites."

"Your faith is important to you," he said.

"It's helped me through some tough times. It can help you, too."

The woman had a kind of courage that mystified Scott. She was still determined to put herself at risk. For him.

That thought made him want to take off, slip out of the resort in the middle of the night and get as far away from Bree as possible. She didn't deserve to be collateral damage to whatever Scott was into.

A knock at the door echoed across the room. Scott got up to answer it. He checked the peephole and spotted Chief Washburn standing outside his door.

"Who is it?" Bree asked.

"The chief." Scott hesitated and glanced at Bree.

She came up beside him and placed a comforting hand on his shoulder.

He wanted to kiss her. In this ridiculously insane moment just before he might be taken away and locked up for good, all he could think about was how soft her lips looked, how much he wanted to taste them.

"You okay?" she said.

He offered a sad smile. "Sure," he said. But he would never be okay because he ached for a woman he could never have.

Scott swung open the door. "Chief, we were expecting the forensic artist."

Chief Washburn nodded at Bree and marched past them into the room. "Can't get one here until tomorrow. I've got good news and bad news."

Scott braced himself against the TV console. Bree came up beside him.

The chief held out a plastic evidence bag with Scott's wallet.

"Your wallet?" Bree said.

Scott nodded, but didn't take his eyes off the chief. The bad news was about to drop. He could feel it.

"That's great," Bree said and glanced at the chief. "Right?"

"You've got two driver's licenses in here, one for Scott James and one for Scott Becket. We ran a background check on Scott Becket and found your employment history with the Chicago P.D. You want to tell me why you checked into the resort using false identification?"

"I have no idea."

"I might be small town, son, but I'm not stupid."

"No, sir, I never thought that."

"Then you'd better come up with some answers, and quick."

"Hang on, the doctors said his concussion was causing his memory loss—"

"Breanna," Chief Washburn said, cutting her off. "You shouldn't even be here so I'd advise you to keep quiet."

She crossed her arms over her chest, obviously not happy with his stern tone. Scott agreed with him: Bree shouldn't be here, especially not now with this new bit of information.

Scott had checked into the resort using an alias, which meant he didn't want to be found. He was running from something, but was it criminal?

"I honestly don't remember anything prior to coming to Washington," Scott said.

"Could it be an undercover assignment?" the chief asked.

Scott shook his head. "It's anybody's guess."

"That's not good enough."

"I understand your position. You need to lock me up, don't you?"

"Wait, you can't." Bree glanced at the chief.

"I can," the chief said, "but I won't until I know what to charge him with other than using a false ID. He could very well be on the job. First thing tomorrow I'm calling the Chicago P.D. In the meantime, do not leave this room."

"Yes, sir," Scott said.

The chief nodded at Bree. "Pack up your things. I'll escort you home."

"But," she started to protest, then acquiesced. "Okay, give me a minute."

"I'll be waiting in the hallway. I need to speak with my officer." Chief Washburn left them alone.

Bree looked at Scott. "I'm sure there's a logical explanation for the ID thing."

"I have no official jurisdiction here."

"There's got to be a good reason for keeping your identity a secret."

He went to the table to help her clean up.

"I have a friend who's an IT genius," she said. "How about I ask him to—"

"No," he said, "let the chief take the lead on this."

For a second he thought she'd argue with him. Instead, she continued to pack up the containers. "I'll leave some brownies and cookies."

He nodded, stuffing the container of macaroni and cheese into the bag. She placed her hand over his and he looked into her amazing green eyes.

"Why don't you call your sister to help you fill in the blanks?" she offered. "You shouldn't be going through this alone."

"So, you're done with me, then?"

"For tonight. I can argue with my brother and win, but the police chief? Don't want to risk getting locked up," she teased. "I'll check on you tomorrow morning, okay?"

"Perhaps it would be safer if you didn't."

"Friends don't abandon each other, Scott."

Slinging her bag over her shoulder, she stepped around the table and hesitated, as if she was about to give him a hug.

The chief knocked on the door. "Ready?" his muffled voice called.

"Coming!" She redirected her attention to Scott. "Be well, and phone your sister."

She reached out and took his hand. "Focus on the goodness in this moment and surrender your heart to God. It will all work out."

With a squeeze of his hand, she smiled, turned and left. The door clicked shut behind her.

He'd never felt more alone in his life, alone and frustrated. He was potentially facing a world of trouble, yet had no means to defend himself, at least not until he remembered why he'd come to Echo Mountain in the first place.

As he went back to finish his sandwich, Bree's satisfied smile flashed across his thoughts. She'd looked so content, almost euphoric when she'd taken a bite of her macaroni. Scott had never experienced that kind of contentment. He'd always been on edge, hyperdiligent about protecting his little sister or making money to pay for clothes growing up. Becoming a cop only fueled his intensity.

Get the bad guy, lock him up, prevent him from hurting innocents.

Innocents like Bree. Scott had to distance himself if he wanted to keep her safe, yet he needed her like nothing he'd ever needed before. No, he only felt this vulnerable and dependent on her because she was offering solace in a raging storm.

Time to reach out for help, something that felt utterly foreign to him. Although he'd lost his cell phone, he did remember Emily's number. He sat on the bed and picked up the receiver.

He got an outside line and made the call. It rang two, three times, and he wondered if Em was out with friends. He glanced at the clock. It was two hours later in Chicago, which mean it was nearly eleven. He worried that he might wake her.

"Hello?" a female voice said.

"Em?"

"Who's this?"

"Her brother, Scott. Who's this and why

are you answering her phone?" He clenched the phone tighter.

"It's her friend Ashley. Emily was in a car accident."

EIGHT

Bree put away the dishes and contemplated a bath with lavender salts and mood-enhancing candles. She loved her nighttime ritual of soaking in the tub while saying her daily prayers. Scott would top the list tonight.

She was about to draw the bath when she realized Fiona hadn't been out since earlier that afternoon. Bree had been so distracted by the day's events she'd neglected her lovable pup.

"Hey, Fi! Let's go potty!" she called, wandering into the living room. Fiona's head perked up from her favorite spot on the couch. "No, I'm not kidding, let's go, silly girl."

Bree grabbed the leash and Fiona catapulted off the couch, rushed Bree and posed in perfect dog sit. "That's my girl."

The bad weather had passed, but fog was

rolling in, giving the resort property an eerie feel. Bree walked Fiona around the perimeter of the property to give her a healthy dose of exercise and a chance to relieve herself. "Such a good girl," Bree praised, as Fiona paced alongside her.

A few minutes later Fiona started whining and pulling on her leash.

"What is it, girl?"

Bree was pretty good at reading Fiona's behavior. A stop usually meant she'd caught an odor, and barking meant she sensed something up ahead. But the whining behavior could mean any number of things. Maybe she sensed a skunk in the woods.

Then the whining grew to a frantic bark. Not excited or pleased, but frantic. Worried.

Bree pulled out her phone and hit the speed dial for Harvey. She didn't call Aiden because she'd had her fill of lectures for the day. Besides, the guy needed to enjoy his time off.

"Bree, everything okay?" Harvey answered.

"Oh, good, you're still on duty. I'm walking Fiona and she's acting rather strange."

"Where are you?"

"South end of the property by the barn."

"I'll check it out."

"I'm sorry to bother you so late with this."

"Don't be. Until I get up the guts to retire, this is part of the job. Go on home."

"Thanks." She ended the call and glanced up ahead. That's when she saw it: the silhouette of a man walking away from the property.

A familiar-looking man.

"Scott!" she called out.

He kept walking. This must be what Fiona was upset about. She sensed Scott's presence and wanted to get to him. Well, so did Bree. She wanted to get to him and find out where he was going and why.

She picked up her pace as she and Fiona jogged toward Scott. He'd turned onto the main road leading to the highway, probably to hitch a ride.

"Scott!" She tried again, but the sound of her voice didn't carry far, so she decided on plan B.

She unleashed Fiona and pointed. "Go get him, girl."

Fiona took off and caught up with Scott, barking and dancing around him. He motioned for her to go away, but Fiona wasn't giving up.

Neither was Bree.

Scott turned around and stuck out his thumb, hoping to catch a ride from an oncoming car. Bree jogged toward him. She knew Fiona wouldn't leave his side, which would surely discourage a motorist from picking him up. One passenger was easy, but a man with a dog? That was messy.

At least that's what Thomas had always said: dogs were messy.

Well, apparently so was love.

Bree was closing in on Scott when a car did, in fact, slow down.

Scott motioned for Fiona to go away.

"Hey, be nice to my dog," she said, out of breath as she caught up to him.

The driver of the car poked his head out the window. It was Will Rankin from SAR.

"Hey Bree, I thought that was Fiona," Will said. "What's she doing out here with this guy?"

Bree smirked at Scott. "She knew he was lost."

"You need a ride back?" Will offered.

"No, we're good, right?" she asked Scott.

"Sure, fine," he said in a low voice.

"Say hi to the girls for me," she said.

"Will do. Be safe."

"You, too."

She commanded Fiona to stand beside her as Will drove off. Bree turned to Scott. "What are you doing out here?"

"Leaving town. But apparently the dog has a better chance of hitching a ride than I do."

"Maybe because you shouldn't be trying to leave. Come on." She took a step in the direction of the resort. Scott didn't move. "Scott?"

"I need to go. My sister was in a car accident."

"Oh, I'm so sorry."

"It's my fault," he said.

"How is that possible? You're here and she's...where is she?"

"Chicago."

"Then it couldn't have been your fault. How is she?"

"Okay, I guess. Her friends are taking turns staying with her."

"Did you speak with your sister?"

"No, she was asleep."

"But no serious injuries?"

"According to her friend Ashley, Em's bruised and sore, but okay."

"Good, that's good." Bree sighed. "And you were headed where, without money or ID?"

"I have to get to her."

"Scott—"

He gripped Bree's arm. "I'm all she's got."

Fiona broke into another round of barking, but this was different than before. Fiona's anxious behavior was warning Scott to release Bree.

"I'm sorry." His fingers sprung free of her arm.

"It's okay," Bree said. "Come on, let's go back."

He glanced at the road ahead with a wistful expression.

"Look, if you leave the resort you'll look guilty of something," Bree said. "You said friends are taking care of your sister. You need to take care of yourself."

Instead, he started to walk toward the main road. This time *she* grabbed *his* arm.

"Stop." She held his gaze. "You won't get

far without money or identification. You're not thinking clearly."

"It's always been my job to take care of her."

"I understand, but sometimes little sisters have to manage on their own. If she knew about your situation she'd want you to focus on your recovery and resolving your situation, right?"

He shrugged.

"Trust me, she would. The best thing you can do for her is to get better and stay safe."

His gaze drifted to the resort, the massive property surrounded by lush forest. "I guess I shouldn't have taken off."

"You were worried about your sister." She took his hand and coaxed him toward the resort. "Give yourself a break. Your brain's still wonky."

"Wonky?"

"You know, wonky, off-kilter."

Once he started walking she was going to let go of his hand, but she sensed he needed the connection, so she held on. Fiona walked alongside them and it struck Bree how normal this looked: a man and woman holding hands, out for a romantic stroll with their dog.

But this wasn't a romantic stroll. This was a rescue mission of sorts.

"So tell me about your sister," Bree said.

"Emily's great." He smiled. "She's two years younger than me, so I've always been protective."

"You're a good older brother."

"I don't know if she'd agree with that. I was pretty bossy when we were kids, but since Mom was always working I was in charge."

"Why'd your mom work so much?"

"Dad left us, didn't offer any financial support so it was up to Mom. When I was old enough I worked and pitched in. It became my job to take care of them." He glanced sideways at her. "How did you do that?"

"Do what?"

"One minute I'm frantic about my sister, the next you've got me telling my life story."

"It's a skill I developed when I did hair in the city. The things people would tell me…" She smiled and shook her head.

"Like what? It's probably a lot more interesting than my life."

"I doubt it. So, you practically raised your sister then what? Did you go to college?"

"Wait a second, is there something more to this line of questioning?"

"Busted." She offered a pleasant smile. "I thought, maybe if we talked about your family and childhood it could help you remember other things."

"Like why I came to Echo Mountain Resort."

"It's worth a try. Anyway, college?"

He glanced up ahead, still holding her hand. "I went to community college, then transferred and got my bachelor's in psychology. I joined the force and became a detective by the time I was thirty."

"Impressive. But you don't think you're still a cop?"

"No." He got a faraway look in his eye, and melancholy creased his brows.

"I'm sorry," she said.

He snapped his attention to her. "For what?"

"My question made you terribly sad."

"I remembered something about a kid being shot, it's a long story. Anyway, I wasn't the same after that. I took a leave of absence and..." His voice trailed off.

"What is it?"

He hesitated. "I took a job in private security."

"When was that?"

"Last year, I think."

"Great, let's figure out who you work for and maybe they'll know why you came to Echo Mountain."

"No, we can't contact them."

"Why not?"

"I'm not sure."

Headlights pierced through the night fog, aimed directly at Bree and Scott. She realized that although they were close to the resort they were still vulnerable out here in the dark.

The car seemed to be going a bit fast for the damp and misty conditions.

"Get behind those trees," Scott said.

"But—"

"Go!"

"Fiona, heel," she said and darted toward the cluster of trees. As she pulled out her phone to call for help, Fiona nudged her and the phone dropped on the ground. "Nuts," she said, running her hands across the damp earth to find it.

"What are you doing out here?" a worried voice shouted.

She recognized it. Harvey.

"It's okay, Harvey!" she called out. "He's with me."

The resort's security manager got out of his truck and peered into the trees. "What are you doing?"

"I saw Scott out here and followed him. He made me take cover when we saw your truck, and now I've lost my phone."

"We thought you were someone else, so I told her hide," Scott said.

"Let's get you two out of here in case that 'someone else' shows up." Harvey walked over to Bree and pointed the flashlight at the ground. In seconds she found the phone.

Bree encouraged Fiona to jump into the flatbed, then she, Scott and Harvey got into the front seat. Harvey spun the truck around and headed for the resort's back entrance closest to Scott's room.

"You were driving awfully fast," Bree said.

"I was worried about your call." Harvey

glanced at her then back at the road. "I won't tell Aiden about this."

"You're the best," Bree said.

"And you—" Harvey aimed a stern look at Scott "—no more late night walkabouts. Got it?"

"Yes, sir."

Harvey parked and escorted them to the door. The cop assigned to watch Scott got out of a nearby squad car and marched up to them wearing an angry frown. "You shouldn't have left the room."

"I know." Scott tapped his head with his fingertips. "The cognitive function is still a little—" he glanced at Bree "—wonky."

"Let's get back inside," the cop said, scanning the property.

Scott nodded at Bree. "Thanks."

"See you tomorrow?"

"Absolutely."

She thought the corner of his lips curled into a slight smile. With a nod, he turned and the cop escorted him inside. Fiona rushed the building, wagging her tail and spying through the glass door for Scott.

"She's developed an attachment to him," Bree said.

"Looks like she's not the only one," Harvey said.

The next morning Scott decided he couldn't continue to live this way, constantly anxious, feeling threatened by the things he didn't remember and therefore couldn't see coming. He also couldn't keep putting Bree at risk. She was the one good thing that had come of this insane situation and he wasn't about to ruin her life because she'd been nice to him.

As he reached for his cup of coffee, he glanced at his hand and remembered how she'd held it last night when she'd stopped him from running away. Running didn't solve problems; it only caused more pain and suffering. Hadn't his father's abandonment taught him anything?

Although it had been Harvey speeding toward them last night, it could have been someone else. Scott was completely vulnerable and helpless until he figured out what had happened during the weeks leading up to his assault in the mountains.

Glancing out the window, he spotted Bree giving directions to a grounds employee. As her gaze roamed the property, it drifted by Scott's window and she smiled, offering an enthusiastic wave. He waved back, remarking how beautiful she looked in her pink fleece jacket and jeans, her blond waves sticking out from a resort baseball cap pulled low to shield her eyes from the sun.

Scott turned away from the window, not wanting to be distracted. He'd awakened this morning with a new goal: piece together his recent past and determine why he'd come to Echo Mountain.

Bree had been on the right track last night. By asking Scott questions and getting him to talk about himself he'd started accessing a part of his brain that could lead him to answers.

Another way to access answers could be through his sister. He needed to call her but had put it off for a full hour, fighting the guilt that he hadn't been there for her, and that somehow her accident had been his fault. Bree had pointed out how implausible that was, but Scott couldn't shake the dread eating away at his gut.

The clock read ten, noon in Chicago. He got an outside line and made the call.

"Hello?"

"Hi, this is Scott, Emily's brother. Who's this?"

"Cassie Marshall, a friend from work. I stopped by to bring lunch."

"How's she doing?"

"Still pretty sore and uncomfortable."

He closed his eyes. His fault, this was his fault. He knew it deep in his core. Somehow his business, his choices had put Em at risk.

"Is she... May I speak with her?"

"Of course, hang on."

He waited a few very long seconds before she came on the line. "Scotty?"

He squeezed the phone at the weak sound of her voice. "Hey, Em, I called last night but Ashley said you were sleeping. I'm sorry I'm not there."

"It's okay, my friends are taking good care of me."

"I should be there."

"No, it's really okay."

"I'm so sorry, kid."

"It happened two days ago. I left you

messages. I thought—" she hesitated "—I thought I'd hear from you sooner."

"I lost my phone."

"Where are you? Ash called your work and they didn't even know."

"Work?"

"Global Resources International."

Okay, now he knew where he'd been working. He jotted it down on a resort notepad.

"Or did you change jobs and not tell me?" Emily asked.

"No, that sounds right."

"It sounds right? Scott, what's going on?"

"I had a hiking accident, hit my head pretty bad and I'm struggling with a mild case of amnesia."

"You're kidding."

"Wish I were."

"Wow, that must be horrible for a control freak like you."

"Control freak, huh?"

"I'm teasing."

But he sensed she wasn't.

"So what happened?" she asked. "Where were you hiking?"

"Cascade Mountains in Washington."

"Why are you out there?"

"Your guess is as good as mine."

"Seriously?"

"I can't remember the accident, or a few months leading up to it. Doctor hopes that will change as the swelling goes down. Anyway, a search-and-rescue team saved me."

More like Breanna McBride saved him.

"Sounds serious if they sent search and rescue to find you. It's just a concussion?"

"And bruised ribs." He didn't want to worry her by mentioning the bullet wound.

"That's a horrible thing to go through by yourself," she said. "I don't know what I'd do without my girlfriends helping me out."

"I'm okay," Scott said. "I've made some friends who are looking after me."

"Don't lie, Scott. It doesn't make me feel better."

"Why do you think I'm lying?"

"Never mind."

"Em?" he pushed.

"You don't do the friend thing, well, except for your partner, Joe. You always said you don't like needing anyone's help, that it makes you weak."

"Well, I'd be a lot weaker without the help I've been getting from the locals."

"Okay, who are you and what have you done with my brother?" she joked.

"Very funny. Tell me about your accident."

"A totally insane driver cuts into my lane and I swerve to avoid a collision, hit a post and the airbag goes off."

"Ouch."

"No kidding. And the jerk didn't even stop. He sped off like he was qualifying for the Indy 500."

"Did you get a good look at the car?"

"A black Lincoln, older model."

The hair pricked on the back of Scott's neck, but he wasn't sure why.

"I gave my statement to the Chicago P.D., so hopefully they'll find the guy. What a jerk. I mean not even stopping to see if I was okay?"

Which meant the driver didn't care if she was okay.

"Scott?"

"Yeah."

"When are you coming back?"

"Not sure. Hopefully soon."

"Are you in trouble?"

"Why do you ask that?"

"I don't know, you seemed more intense

than usual these past few months, and now you sound—" she paused "—strange."

"I'm worried about you."

"Don't be. I'm a big girl and my friends are totally smothering me."

Cassie said something in the background to drive the point home.

"I'm glad you called," Emily said. "When you didn't come by to check on me or call I got worried. I thought…"

"You thought I'd left, like him."

"No, I thought—"

"It's okay. I should be there and I'm not."

"Scotty—"

"You should have the number of the resort I'm staying at. Got a piece of paper?"

"No, but I can have Cassie write it down."

"Good. Call if anything changes."

"Sure, okay. Here's Cassie." Emily passed the phone to her friend and Scott gave her the phone number for the resort and his room number.

"Cassie, I can't tell you how much I appreciate you guys taking care of my sister."

"We're happy to do it. That's what friends are for. Bye."

Scott hung up and stared at the phone,

concern flooding his chest. Whatever he'd been working on caused the hit-and-run accident that hurt his sister. He could feel it in his gut. But what could he do about it from two thousand miles away?

Friends.

Scott considered calling the one person who'd been there for him when he was on the job: his partner. He slowly pressed the buttons to call Joe, surprised that he remembered the number since he hadn't used it in months. He knew his former partner had a thing for Emily, and Scott hoped those feelings would override whatever resentment Joe felt about Scott leaving the force and abandoning his partner.

"Detective Rush," he answered.

"Joey, it's Scott."

Silence.

"Joe?" Scott pressed.

"What?"

"I need a favor."

"You have *got* to be kidding."

"It's not for me. It's about Emily."

"What about her?"

"She was in a hit-and-run. I think it was intentional."

"Yeah, right, like anyone would want to hurt that sweet girl."

"They were trying to send me a message."

"Great, what did you get yourself into, Mr. hotshot security goon?"

"Joey—"

"I've been waiting for this call, the one where you'd admit you were wrong, that you shouldn't have left the department, but this? You put your sister at risk? What's the matter with you?"

"Joe, I—"

"It's always about you, isn't it? The self-judgment, the blame. You act like you're the only one who was affected by that kid's death, Scott. Aw, forget it."

The line went dead.

"Joey?"

Scott sighed. His former partner had hung up on him. Maybe Scott deserved it, but he hoped the resentment Joe felt for him wouldn't prevent him from checking on Em.

Scott was banking on the fact that the many years of friendship he'd shared with Joe counted for something, because the thought of someone stalking and hurting Emily…

"Please, God," he whispered and caught himself. He wasn't one to lean on God, yet Bree drew so much strength from her faith. It fascinated him. Right now Scott felt so helpless about both his sister's situation and his own personal safety.

He opened the nightstand drawer and pulled out the Bible. Turning to a random page, he landed on *Psalm* 57.

"Be merciful and gracious to me, O God, be merciful *and* gracious to me, for my soul takes refuge *and* finds shelter *and* confidence in You; yes, in the shadow of Your wings I will take refuge *and* be confident until calamities *and* destructive storms have passed."

Someone knocked on the door, probably Bree coming to check on him. He placed the Bible on the nightstand, went to the door and glanced through the peephole. A resort employee stood outside his door.

Scott cracked it open. "Yes?"

"Room service."

Scott glanced at two covered plates on the cart. "I didn't order anything."

"A friend ordered for you, sir," the man said. "She'll be joining you shortly."

Scott smiled to himself. Even when she wasn't here Bree was taking care of him. He'd be able to dive into his investigation more effectively on a full stomach, so he swung open the door and the employee wheeled the cart inside.

Scott glanced up and down the hall, wondering what happened to his shadow cop. Truth was he didn't need full-time surveillance. Like Bree had said, he couldn't get far without a driver's license, money or credit cards.

"Sorry, I don't have my wallet so I can't offer a tip," Scott said, closing the door.

"That's okay, sir. I don't want your money." The guy pulled the cover off a plate and turned.

He was pointing a gun at Scott.

Scott automatically raised his hands.

"I'm surprised you let me in," the man said. He was in his sixties with salt-and-pepper hair and a square jaw. "Although you seemed a little distracted when you were eyeing the hallway. Looking for the cute blonde?"

Scott glared. "I don't know who you're talking about."

"Uh-huh."

This must be one of the guys who'd assaulted Scott in the mountains…and was here to finish the job.

"What do you want?" Scott said.

"Sit." He jerked the barrel of the gun sideways.

Scott sat at the table and lowered his hands.

"You know what I want," the guy said. "The water samples."

Scott had no idea what he was talking about. Now what? He decided to use the truth as his defense.

"Guess you haven't heard, I'm suffering from retrograde amnesia," Scott said.

"Right, and I'm Frosty the Snowman."

"You said yourself that I should have known better than to let you in. Do I know you? Because if I do, I can't remember."

"No kidding," he said, sarcasm lacing his voice. "Okay, I'll play along. You can call me Rich, although that's obviously not my real name. So, Scott, how about you tell me where you stashed the water samples and I'll leave you alone."

"I told you, I can't remember."

Someone tapped on the door. "Scott? It's Bree."

Scott tensed, his eyes glancing at the door, then back at his attacker.

"Maybe she can help you remember," Rich said with a wicked smile.

He must have read the fear on Scott's face. "Ask her to join us."

"Scott?" She knocked again. "You okay?"

"Well, go on, lover boy," Rich said.

Scott went to the door and placed his hand against the heavy steel. He had to do something to drive her away, and fast.

"I'm not decent."

"But I just saw—"

"Leave me alone!" he shouted.

Silence answered him. His heart ached at the thought that her last memory of Scott would be his cruel tone, since his attacker surely wasn't going to let him live. She disappeared from the peephole. Relief coursed through him.

Without warning, Rich slugged Scott in

his bruised ribs. Scott doubled over and fell to his knees, gasping for breath.

"Smart guy, huh?" He leaned close. "It's time you gave up your crusade."

Scott couldn't give the guy what he wanted, but at least he knew he'd been up in the mountains taking water samples for some mysterious reason.

"Maybe if I knock you around, that brain of yours will get back on track." The guy swung the gun at Scott's head.

NINE

Bree jerked away from the door, the hair bristling on the back of her neck.

Scott was in trouble, big-time.

She took off for the security office, hoping to find Harvey, or even her brother. Aiden would probably brush her off, saying she was too sensitive and a man yelling at her to go away wasn't cause for alarm.

But it was. Bree had seen a staff member roll a food cart into Scott's room, so when she knocked on the door only moments later and he claimed he wasn't decent, she knew something was wrong.

Then he yelled at her.

A small part of her brain argued that he'd had enough of Bree, but she shoved that thought aside and focused on helping him.

She rounded the corner at a fast clip and

nearly collided with a tall man in a suit walking beside her brother.

"Where's the officer watching Scott?" she asked Aiden.

"This is Officer Willet. I asked them to nix the uniforms so their presence wouldn't alarm guests."

She looked at Officer Willet with pleading eyes. "Scott's in trouble."

"Isn't Officer Jones guarding his room?"

"No. Come on."

The three of them approached Scott's door and the cop motioned for Bree and Aiden to stand aside.

"Why do you think he's in trouble?" Officer Willet asked.

"I just know."

The cop pounded on the door. "Scott, it's Officer Willet. I need to go over a few things with you. Please open the door."

The cop waited. Bree interlaced her fingers together and squeezed.

"Why do you think he's in trouble?" Aiden pressed.

"Because he yelled at me," she admitted.

"Bree," Aiden said in that shaming tone.

She stared directly into his sky-blue eyes.

"I know he's in trouble the same way you knew I was in trouble back in Seattle, so don't mess with me."

A crash echoed from the room, then something slammed against the door.

"Key." The plainclothes cop stuck out his hand.

Aiden handed him a master key, and shifted Bree out of harm's way.

"Stay back," Officer Willet said.

The cop withdrew his firearm, swiped the key card and tried opening the door, but something was blocking it. The cop pushed harder and the door swung open. Officer Willet bolted into the room.

"Patio," Scott's voice gasped.

Bree slipped inside before the door closed. The officer rushed out the sliding doors to the patio, and Aiden followed close behind, but didn't go outside. He stood at the glass door barking orders into his radio.

"Bree?"

She glanced down to her left. Scott was sitting against the wall, clutching his rib cage.

"What happened?" She kneeled beside him and searched his eyes.

"You got help?" he said. "After I yelled at you?"

"I knew you didn't mean it."

He tipped his head back against the wall and sighed. "Thank you."

"Where are you hurt?" she said.

"What happened in here?" Aiden said, sliding the glass doors shut and glancing around the disheveled room.

"They sent a guy in a room service uniform to get information out of me," Scott said.

"What kind of information?" Aiden stepped closer.

"Back off, big brother. Let's get him some ice for his ribs," Bree said.

Her brother was wearing that determined look, that *I'm not going to let anyone hurt my baby sister* look.

"It's okay," Scott said, and slowly got up. Bree helped him across the room to sit at the table. "He asked me where I stashed the water samples."

"What water samples?" Aiden asked.

"Have no idea, but at least I have more information than I did yesterday. I found out who I work for, and apparently I have water samples worth killing for. I'll spend the afternoon looking into it. I've got a laptop around here somewhere."

"I can help," Bree said.

"Don't you have to finish putting up Christmas decorations on the south end of the property?" Aiden questioned.

"It's my official day off."

"Bree—"

"The sooner I help Scott figure this out the sooner he'll be gone. That's what you want, right?" she challenged.

"Mr. McBride, this is Justin in Facilities, over," a voice squawked through Aiden's radio.

"Go ahead, Justin." Aiden spoke into his radio, but didn't take his eyes off Bree.

"We've got a problem in the D wing, sir. I think you'd better come."

"On my way." Aiden sighed. "Be careful," he said to Bree.

"I will."

He pointed his radio at Scott. "And no more room service."

"He has to eat," Bree protested.

"I'll send something down for lunch and

dinner, but don't answer unless they say it's from me, got it?" Aiden said.

"Okay," Bree said.

Aiden reached for the door.

"Hey, Aiden?" Scott said.

Aiden turned.

"Thanks," Scott said.

With a curt nod, Aiden left.

Scott looked at Bree. "I think he's starting to like me."

"Uh-huh, he'll probably invite you to Christmas dinner," she said teasingly.

"I make a mean cranberry sauce."

"I'll bet." She examined a cut on his cheek. "How does it look, doc?"

"We should wash it out. You want ice for the ribs?"

"Probably a good idea."

"I'll have the concierge send it over."

"I need to find my laptop." He glanced around the room, as if trying to remember where he'd stashed it.

His curious expression grew frustrated.

"Check the closet," she suggested. "I'll call for the ice."

She called Nia at the concierge desk and ordered ice. Scott searched the closet slowly, as if he didn't recognize his own clothes. He had at least five shirts hanging in the closet, so he'd planned on being here nearly a week.

If he was collecting water samples that could be from the bigger lakes, like Lake Stevens or smaller lakes hidden in the mountains. What she couldn't figure out was why he needed water samples in the first place.

"Are you working for the EPA?" she asked.

He shut the closet door and turned to her. "What?"

"Is that why you need water samples?"

"I don't know." He opened the top drawer on the dresser and moved clothes around. "Here it is."

Laptop in hand, he shifted into a chair at the table and winced.

"I've got pain relievers in my purse," she said, joining him at the table.

"No, I'm good."

"You don't look good."

He glanced up. "Gee, thanks."

"I meant, you look like you're hurting." She certainly didn't mean it the other way, although the truth was she found Scott incredibly handsome. Heat flushed her cheeks in an unwelcome blush.

"What's wrong?" he asked.

"Nothing." She stood and went to the bathroom. "I'm getting a washcloth to clean out your cut."

"Okay, but then I have a job for you."

A job other than nursing him back to health and helping him get his life back? Sure, she would nurse the wounded bird so that he'd be strong enough to fly away. That's what she was doing, right? It's not as though she could have any kind of relationship with this man once he got his memory and his life back.

She ran a white washcloth under warm water and studied her reflection in the bathroom mirror. It was a shame that they'd met under such dire circumstances because she felt a true connection to Scott, an honest connection.

Then again, maybe that was due to his vulnerability. She knew that some confident men—men like Thomas—pushed and shoved until they had you cornered and helpless, willing to do whatever they wanted. Even her brother tended to be bossy and overbearing although she understood he was motivated by brotherly love.

At any rate, she'd appreciate whatever time she had with Scott, helping him resolve his situation and get his life back. She wrung out the washcloth and went into the room. Scott intently studied something on his laptop.

"What'd you find?" she asked, shifting a chair close to him.

She pressed the washcloth against his facial cut. He closed his eyes and she snapped her hand back. "Sorry, does that hurt?"

"No, it feels good."

She continued to clean the wound. It was a small cut, but the skin around it was red and angry. "How's the arm?"

"It's fine."

She dabbed at his cheek for a few seconds, then sat back in the chair. "I think you're good."

"Am I?" he asked, searching her eyes.

It seemed as though he was going to kiss her.

"Scott, I…"

He pressed his forefinger to her lips. "I need to say something, and I've probably said it before, but it's worth repeating." He hesitated. "Breanna, I don't know what I'd do without you right now. I needed you to know that."

"I'm glad I could be here for you."

And I'm starting to care about you, a lot.

She couldn't say the words, words that seemed trite considering they'd known each other only a few days.

"I wish…" he started.

"What?"

He took the washcloth out of her hand and brought her fingers to his lips. A shiver of warmth crept down her spine. She loved the feel of his lips pressed against her knuckles. It was such a delicate, tender touch.

"When this is all over," he said, "maybe we could catch a movie or something?" He looked up, hopeful.

"Even a romantic comedy?"

He smiled. "Sure."

"Wow, I'm impressed."

Someone knocked on the sliding door. "It's Officer Willet," the muffled voice said.

Scott opened the door and let him in.

"He's gone," the cop said. "I'll call it in to the chief. He wanted to be kept in the loop. What'd the guy look like?"

"Older guy, salt-and-pepper hair. Called

himself Rich, but said that wasn't his real name." Scott walked him to the door.

"That sounds like the man I saw at the hospital," Bree said.

"Apparently the assailant had a partner who lured Officer Jones away from his post," Officer Willet said.

"Is Officer Jones okay?" Bree asked.

"He's fine." Officer Willet turned to Scott. "Keep the slider and this door locked and secure."

"Yes, sir."

Scott closed the door and double-locked it, then joined Bree at the table. "I shouldn't have let Rich get away."

"You were working at a slight disadvantage."

"That's no excuse."

"Let's focus on what we *can* do." She glanced at the laptop. "You were about to come up with a plan?"

"I got the name of my employer from Emily. I should call and find out what I was working on. Maybe they sent me out here. But it feels strange to call about myself."

"I can call," Bree offered. "What do you want me to say?"

"Ask for me, see if you can find out where I am and when I'm supposed to return."

"Don't you want to speak with your boss and ask him directly?"

His brows furrowed as if he was remembering something. "It's not a good idea. I'm not sure why."

She picked up the phone. "What's the number?"

He handed her the resort notepad with a number on it. That's when she noticed the Bible sitting out on the nightstand. That was certainly a good sign.

She made the call and when the receptionist picked up she asked for Scott Becket's extension. A few rings later a woman answered. "Security."

"Hi, I'm looking for Scott Becket."

"May I ask who's calling?"

"Breanna McBride."

"Hold on."

Bree put her hand over the mouthpiece. "She's acting like you're there and she's going to put me through."

"This is Sue Percy," a woman said. "Scott is out of the office for a few weeks. Can I help you?"

"No, thanks, I'm a friend and wanted to catch up."

"When was the last time you spoke with Scott?"

"Why do you ask?"

"Hang on." A few seconds passed and Bree thought she heard a door shut in the background. Sue came back on the line. "We've been worried about him. He disappeared two weeks ago and hasn't called in."

"Oh, that's odd."

"I know he had vacation time coming, but to leave so suddenly was strange, and then some money went missing from petty cash."

"How much money?"

There was a long pause, then, "I need to go. Goodbye."

The line went dead. "O-kay."

"Why did you ask about money?" Scott said.

"The woman said you stopped coming into work about the same time petty cash went missing."

"What?" Scott stood and paced the room. "That's ridiculous. How much?"

"She wouldn't say."

"Why would I steal from my employer?"

"Don't assume you did."

"But she said—"

"It didn't sound like she thought you stole the money. It sounded like she was touting the company line."

"You got that from one phone call?" he asked.

"I've got good instincts."

Scott iced his ribs and was going through his laptop for clues when the forensic artist showed up. Scott and Bree worked with the artist on a sketch of the man who'd tried forcing Breanna into his car yesterday. By the time the artist was done, Scott felt as though he'd drawn a good likeness of the guy.

"That's pretty good," Scott said.

The forensic artist looked at Bree for confirmation.

"Yes, that looks like him."

The man who'd almost abducted Bree.

Scott balled his hand into a fist and tapped it against his thigh. Bree escorted the artist to the door and thanked him for his service.

Scott wanted answers. He wanted this whole thing over so he could be sure Bree was safe from harm, because by now it was clear she was in this for the long haul and nothing would dissuade her from staying close.

Which was even more motivation for Scott to remember what had brought him here.

He clicked through files on his computer, looking for anything that seemed even remotely related to water, but found nothing. He opened a file titled Lake Trip 2013 and thumbnail photos popped up on the screen. He clicked one open: it was a shot of Scott with his arm around an attractive redhead in a bathing suit. Christa. Right, his...girlfriend?

"What'd you find?" Bree said, approaching him.

"Nothing important. Vacation pictures." He clicked the picture closed. "There's got to be something on here that can help us."

He clicked open his email account and scanned through his sent folder. "Check this out, an email dated three weeks ago scheduling time off."

As Bree read the email over his shoulder, he inhaled her floral scent. He loved the way she smelled, the way she absently placed her hand on his shoulder as she peered at the screen.

"Open that one," she said, and pointed.

He clicked open an email from the human resources manager approving his time off.

"Okay, so if they approved it, why did Sue Percy say you mysteriously disappeared?"

"I can't trust anyone at work," he said.

"Maybe not, but you could retrace your steps."

She let her hand slip off his shoulder and sat next to him at the table. "Let's figure out where you went from the time you arrived in town until we rescued you."

"How are we going to do that?"

"It's a small town. Trust me, if someone spotted a handsome stranger like you, they'd make a mental note. Plus, when we get your wallet back from Chief Washburn we can go online and check your credit card activity."

"If he gives it back."

"It's not evidence unless a crime's been committed, right?"

"It's called fraud."

She leaned back in her chair and sighed.

He hated that she looked so frustrated. Then a thought struck him. "Hang on, you're on the right track," he said. "How about we start here, at the resort? This place has video surveillance. I noticed it last night. Let's ask Harvey if we can see video from the day I checked in."

"What are you thinking?"

"We'll start at the beginning and build a time line. In the meantime, you can reach out to folks in the community and see if they spotted me and if so, what I was doing."

"Sounds good. I'll start with Mom's book group. They meet every other week. They're pretty tuned into what's happening in town. First I'll call Harvey."

She stood and went to dig her phone out of her purse.

Scott redirected his attention to his laptop. Something in here had to offer a clue as to why he had water samples and who wanted them. Sifting through a few files, it became apparent he was in personal security for Phillip Oppenheimer, owner of Global Resources International—GRI. Scott found daily activity logs that outlined which security agents would be shadowing Phillip and his senior managers. There were at least two bodyguards assigned to the CEO at any given time. Scott wondered why a CEO would need such tight security.

He did an internet search on GRI and a few news stories popped up. Apparently Phillip Oppenheimer was some kind of genius and his company had developed a refinery that converted various types of waste products into diesel fuel.

"Thanks, Harvey," Bree said and turned to Scott, pocketing her phone. "Harvey said as a personal favor to me, he'd let us review the video."

"That's good, that's good," he said, distracted by an article on Global Resources International.

"What'd you find?" She sat beside him again.

"I work for one of the top guys in alternative energy development."

"Nice."

"Maybe I was investigating a competitor or someone who was trying to put him out of business?"

"Could be. What kind of energy?"

"A refining process that turns waste into diesel fuel."

"Wow, that's amazing. I wonder if that has something to do with the new plant up north."

"New plant?" He glanced at her.

"It opened earlier this year, but they didn't hire any locals. We all thought that was weird, but apparently it's automated and needs very few employees to run effectively."

"Huh." He clicked on the GRI website and found a page that identified their production locations. "Is it in Wallace County?"

"Yep."

"That's twenty miles north of here. So, if I'm investigating something related to the plant, what would I be doing in Echo Mountain?"

"Well, there aren't many hotels near the plant."

"Right, but the day you found me I was hiking in Woods Pass, nowhere near the plant. If I could get up to Wallace County and do a little digging..." He sighed. "I need to find my rental car."

"You could call the park service and ask

if any cars have been abandoned in the past three days."

A knock echoed across the room.

"Aiden must have sent lunch," she said, getting up to answer the door.

He touched her arm. "No, I'll get it. You stay back."

As Scott went to the door, his mind clicked off possible reasons why he was here in Washington and didn't want to call his boss to tell him what was happening. Scott probably didn't want to disappoint him and risk losing his coveted position. Memories began to surface, like the boost to Scott's confidence when Mr. Oppenheimer had hired him to lead his security team. Scott hadn't want him to think he'd made a mistake by putting Scott in charge.

He glanced into the peephole and saw Chief Washburn.

"It's not lunch," Scott said to Bree, then opened the door. "Good morning, Chief."

Chief Washburn marched into the room and turned to Scott. "The gun you found in your room?" He glanced at Bree, then back at Scott.

Scott pressed his back against the door, bracing himself.

"Go on," Scott said.

"It was used in a shooting two months ago."

TEN

Bree wouldn't believe Scott had anything to do with a shooting, but she knew better than to argue with the chief, so she kept quiet.

"Was anyone killed?" Scott said in a defeated tone.

"No fatalities."

Scott sighed. "So you're taking me in, after all?"

"No."

Scott glanced up.

"The gun wasn't registered to you and the shootings were gang-related so I'm mystified as to how the weapon ended up in your room. It's almost like someone planted it here."

"If it isn't my gun, whose is it?"

Chief Washburn pulled out a small notebook. "It was registered to an Arthur Brown of Chicago, but he reported it stolen a year ago. You know him?"

"No, sir, I don't think so."

"There's more." Washburn consulted his notebook. "I spoke with detective Joe Rush at the Chicago P.D.—"

"My ex-partner."

"He said Scott James was your undercover alias. You left the department last year to work in private security after the death of a teenager."

The frozen expression of Miguel Domingo still haunted Scott.

"You were cleared of any wrongdoing," the chief added.

Which didn't ease the guilt, guilt for not solving the case fast enough.

"A few months ago the chief of detectives asked Detective Rush for your contact information. When I called to inquire about your alias, Rush said maybe the chief has you working on something." Chief Washburn studied Scott. "Does this ring any bells?"

Scott shook his head. "I wish I could help."

"I've left a message for the chief to get back to me and your partner vouched for you. Apparently you're a good cop." Chief

Washburn pulled Scott's wallet out of his jacket pocket. "You can have this back, but use your real identification from now on, okay?"

"Yes, sir. So, am I free to leave the premises?"

"I suppose I can't stop you. That said, I'd rather not have you running around town with guys using you as target practice." The chief glanced at Bree. "And I surely don't want her getting caught in the cross fire."

"No sir, that won't happen."

"You sound awfully sure of yourself."

"I am, sir. Like you said, I was—" he paused "—a good cop. I'll keep her safe. But I have to get out and conduct an investigation in order to solve this."

"I wish I could offer some help, but we're strapped for manpower as it is. I had to borrow from the reserves to keep an eye on you."

"And I appreciate that, sir."

"Where will you start your investigation?"

"First I'm going to retrace my steps beginning with the day I checked into the resort."

With a nod, the chief walked toward the

door. "Good plan. But do not go into those mountains without backup."

"You just said you were strapped for manpower."

The chief turned to Scott. "I'll figure something out if you plan to head back up there. We've got some professional climbers in law enforcement who'd jump at the chance to accompany you."

"Thank you, sir."

"Be safe," the chief said, and nodded at Bree.

"Bye, Chief," she said.

Scott turned to Bree, pressing the heel of his palm against his temple.

"Hey, what's wrong?" She went to him.

"Headache's back. Maybe all that computer work." He went to the bed and stretched out on top of the covers.

"I'll get a cool washcloth. When was the last time you took an aspirin?"

"Last night."

"Well, you need one of those, but you should probably have food first. I'll call Aiden."

Scott draped his hand over his face. Bree worried about him, worried that the headache had consumed him so quickly. Perhaps this warranted a trip back to the E.R. After all, the stranger's attack this morning could have exacerbated his head injury.

First things first. She hit speed dial on her phone and called her brother.

"Yes, Bree," Aiden answered, his voice clipped.

"You okay?"

"Toilet broke in 337 and water's been leaking two floors into the rooms below. Not a fun morning."

"Oh, I'm sorry. Is it okay if I order room service for Scott and me? I know you said you were going to, but you sound busy."

"Sure, go ahead. Ask Nia to personally bring it to your room, that way you'll know it's legit."

"Will do. Chief Washburn stopped by with good news. He confirmed with Chicago P.D. that Scott's a good cop, so you can stop worrying about me."

"Sorry, kid, that ain't happening. Gotta go."

"Good luck."

"Thanks, you, too."

She hung up and smiled to herself. Well,

at least their conversation was more pleasant than the last time they spoke. She didn't like being at odds with her brother, but wasn't sure how to get him to ease up on the over-protectiveness.

"What do you want for lunch?" she said, glancing at Scott.

"Whatever you're having."

"Soup and sandwich okay?"

"Sounds good."

She placed the order with Nia and asked her to deliver the cart personally. While they waited for lunch, Bree ran a washcloth under cool water and placed it on Scott's forehead.

"How's that?" she asked.

"Good, better." He reached up and placed his hand over hers. "I hate feeling so weak."

"It's okay. Listen to your body. It wants to heal."

"I wish it would heal faster."

"You shouldn't push it. Maybe we should take it easy this afternoon. Not do any running around."

"Can't. Have to figure this out," he said, sounding a little anxious.

"We will, we will," she hushed.

Bree started humming, but this time it

wasn't to calm herself. She hoped the sound might give Scott a little peace.

"I know that one," he said, his voice soft.

She realized she was humming "Silent Night," which had been one of her favorites since she was a little girl.

A few minutes later Scott's hand slid off of Bree's and landed on the pillow beside his head. He'd fallen asleep.

"Rest, my friend. Rest and heal." Bree hummed beside him for a bit. She removed the cloth from his forehead and placed the back of her hand against his skin. He wasn't overly hot, so she didn't think he was running a fever.

After rinsing the washcloth under cool water yet again, she reapplied it to Scott's forehead and closed her eyes to say a silent prayer. *Dear God, thank You for this moment of peace, amen.*

Gratitude prayers always seemed to bring balance to a tenuous situation. Even in her worst days under Thomas's thumb, she'd find things to be grateful for: a sun break on a cloudy Seattle day or a little girl pushing her doll in a buggy alongside her mom.

Gratitude kept Bree sane during an emotional whirlwind of turmoil.

Eyeing Scott, she wondered what things he had to be grateful for. She sensed there was darkness in his past, but she hoped he'd be able to focus on the light, which would surely help him heal faster.

After a few minutes, she decided to continue his investigation by going through some of the files on his laptop. Since the eyestrain might have spiked Scott's headache, she'd save him that discomfort and take over the project.

She positioned herself at the table and noticed he hadn't signed out of his email. Scanning his inbox, she spotted one from a rental car agency. Apparently he'd reserved a mid-size car for pickup at Sea-Tac airport over a week ago. She jotted down the phone number of the agency and the confirmation number. She'd call to determine what type of car he actually drove off in that day, which would then help them track it down.

Someone tapped at the door. If it was Nia with lunch, that certainly was quick.

She went to the door, glanced through the peephole and spotted Uncle Chuck pacing in the hallway. Terrific. She didn't need another lecture, but wouldn't be rude.

Bree snatched a key card from the nightstand and went to the door. She didn't want to wake Scott.

She stepped into the hallway and quietly shut the door behind her. "Hey, Uncle Chuck."

"Your mom's been worried about you so I said I'd stop by the resort."

"I'm fine, thanks. I talked to Mom last night."

"She told me you're still hanging out with trouble in there."

"He's a cop, maybe on an undercover assignment. Ask Chief Washburn, he'll explain it."

"It's not appropriate."

"Uh, what isn't appropriate?"

"Whatever you're doing with him in there."

"I was putting a cool washcloth on his forehead and humming a Christmas song. He's still suffering from headaches thanks to the concussion."

"*He* is not *your* problem," he said in a firm voice.

She clenched her jaw against the shame crawling down her back. But this was Uncle Chuck trying to make Bree's mom happy by checking on her daughter. This wasn't about control or manipulation or—

"You need to stay away from him," he continued. "You don't know what he's into or who will come after him next. I heard about the room service incident, and you were standing right outside the door. You could have been seriously hurt."

"But I wasn't. Scott protected me."

"Don't be absurd."

Bree tried not to let the harsh words affect her, but she got that shrinking feeling again, the one that made her feel small and foolish.

No. No one was allowed to make her feel that way again.

She planted her hands on her hips. "I appreciate your concern but this is my business, Uncle Chuck. If Mom has a problem with how I'm conducting myself, she'll let me know."

"She'll be devastated if anything happens to you and it's my job to make sure it doesn't."

"Actually, it's mine," she said with a lift of her chin. "I'm responsible for myself, my decisions and actions."

"You're not thinking straight. That ex-boyfriend of yours has you twisted all up inside."

"Excuse me?" she said, horrified by the reminder.

Uncle Chuck must have realized he'd crossed the line. He sighed and leaned back. "I'm sorry, but I don't think you know what kind of people you're dealing with here."

"Hi, Bree," Nia called as she wheeled a cart toward them.

The concierge couldn't have come at a better time. Bree had had enough of Uncle Chuck's criticism and lectures. He meant well, but his delivery was hurtful.

"Hey, Nia," Bree said, turning to her friend. "Thanks for bringing lunch."

"My pleasure. Hey, Chief," she greeted Uncle Chuck. Most resort employees knew him because Chuck would bring Mom to the resort for dinner a few times a month.

Nia rolled up to the door and waited for Bree to open it.

"He's resting so I'll take it inside," Bree said.

"Great." Nia eyed Uncle Chuck. "What brings you to the resort, Chief?"

"Checking on my friend, here." He nodded at Bree.

"I appreciate the visit," Bree said. "I'll call Mom later." She swiped the key card and pushed the cart into Scott's room. She grabbed the door before it slammed shut, and eased it closed.

With a frustrated sigh, she wheeled the cart next to the dining table. Mom hadn't seemed overly worried last night when they spoke, certainly not worried enough to send Chuck to check on Bree.

Maybe it was Chuck's way of earning points with his girl, at least that's how he liked to think of Margaret McBride. Bree suspected Mom didn't consider her relationship with Chuck a serious one. Mom had shied away from romance ever since Dad passed away, saying she was blessed with true love once and didn't need to go looking for more.

True love. Did it exist in Bree's future? She'd pretty much given up on love after the disaster with Thomas. That nasty experience had proven to Bree that she had the worst judgment where men and love were concerned.

She glanced over her shoulder at Scott—still sound asleep. Talk about bad judgment. She could feel herself starting to care about him more than she should, yet she knew the unrealistic nature of their relationship. She took care of him during a frightening and vulnerable time. After this was over, he'd move back to Chicago and forget all about her.

He may have asked her out for a future date, but she couldn't count on him following through once he got his life back. Still, it was a nice gesture.

She pushed the curtain aside and spotted Ruby, one of the grounds crew, stringing Christmas lights along the split rail fence. The wrong lights. Rats, Aiden had given her specific instructions and she thought she'd clearly explained them to her coworkers. She'd better correct the issue before Aiden got on her case about neglecting her job.

Scott would probably nap for a while, giving Bree time to speak with Ruby and return without him noticing she was gone. Just in case, she left the bottle of pain reliever on the table and wrote him a note. She placed it prominently on the laptop and headed out.

The shrill sound of a siren tweaked his eardrums. Scott opened his eyes and glanced up at the gray sky. Light flakes of snow dropped into his face as he lay flat on his back.

"Help me, somebody help me," a soft, high-pitched voice said.

Scott couldn't move. It was like his body was glued to the pavement.

"Please, won't somebody help?"

He turned his head to the right... .

And spotted Miguel Domingo, looking exactly the way he did that cold February night when Scott found him in the street, shot by a gang member's bullet.

A gut-wrenching sob caught in the back of Scott's throat. Why did the kid have to get involved? Scott told him he'd find evidence against the guys who killed his brother, but Miguel couldn't wait.

"How could you let me die?" Miguel said.

"Why, Scott, why?" a female voice said from the other side of Scott.

With great effort, he turned his head to the left....

Bree's beautiful green eyes stared at him. She wore a confused and desperate frown.

"Bree?" he said.

The siren grew louder, the sound making his eyes water with pain. Then Breanna blinked twice and her eyes stayed open with the blank stare of a corpse.

"No!"

Scott sat up, gasping for breath. Searching his surroundings, he struggled to figure out where he was and what just happened. He was damp with sweat and his head pounded. That's when he realized the phone was ringing on the nightstand beside his bed.

Sitting up, he grabbed the receiver. "Yeah?"

"Amnesia? Really?" his ex-partner said.

"Joe?"

"I spoke with the Echo Mountain police chief. So, you're working an undercover gig? For who? I thought you were off the payroll."

"I'm not sure."

"I get it. Need to know stuff. It's cool. I'll stop by your sister's this afternoon."

"Thanks man, thanks," Scott said with as much gratitude as he could muster.

"You think her accident is related to what you're working on out there?"

"It's possible, I'm not sure. My head's still foggy from the assault, and then some guy came after me this morning and whacked me pretty hard."

"Good thing you've got a head like a rock."

"Yeah."

"About before, that stuff I said about abandoning the job—"

"It's fine," Scott interrupted, because he wasn't so sure he hadn't done just that. Scott was confused about some things, but he didn't think his current investigation was part of an undercover assignment.

"Gotta run," Joe said.

"Thanks for calling, Joey."

"Yep."

Scott hung up and stretched out his neck. The headache wasn't as bad as it was earlier thanks to Bree stroking his head with a cool cloth.

Bree. The nightmare.

Panic clenched his gut. He glanced around the room and spotted a note on his laptop. A room service cart was positioned next to the table.

He wondered where she'd gone, but he had no right to expect her to stay close, to continue sitting beside him and stroking his forehead, humming "Silent Night." Yet anxiety tangled his insides whenever she was gone.

He had to figure out how to stop that; stop being so dependent on this woman.

He went to the table and read the note. She was helping an employee with Christmas lights and would be back shortly. Scott downed a few aspirin that she'd left for him. Curious, he took the metal cover off the room service plate to reveal a turkey sandwich. He checked the other one, as well, also turkey. So, she'd left without eating?

The phone rang again. He went to answer it, hoping it was Bree. "I have to let go of this," he muttered, then ripped the phone off the cradle. "Hello?"

Silence answered him.

"Hello?" he tried again.

"You know what we want," a deep voice said. "You've got twenty-four hours."

He gripped the phone. "I can't help you. I can't remember—"

"Figure it out or we'll end that pretty blonde nurse of yours."

Click.

Scott had to get to Bree, warn her and protect her. But how when he didn't even know where she'd gone? She could be stringing lights anywhere on the property.

He called the front desk and asked to be put through to security, hoping Harvey would know her location, but his voice mail picked up.

He grabbed his jacket and a key card off the table and rushed out.

Heart racing, Scott sprinted to the nearest exit and shoved open the door. A cool blast of winter air shocked him fully awake. He glanced up at the gray sky: it looked like snow was about to fall.

Scott scanned the property and noticed an employee stringing lights along a wooden fence. Jogging toward her, Scott's eyes kept moving, seeking out Bree, hoping he'd find her safe and unharmed.

"Good afternoon!" he called out.

The young woman turned to him. She was in her twenties with fair skin and red hair. Her name tag read Ruby.

"Can I help you?" Ruby asked with a smile.

"I'm looking for Bree."

"She was here a minute ago. I think she went to find replacement bulbs for the ones that burned out."

"Where would she have gone to get replacement bulbs?"

"Either the barn, or in the storage locker by the security office."

"Where's that?"

"Inside the south entrance." She pointed.

"Thanks." Scott headed toward the building, shoving his hands in his jacket pockets, focused on finding Bree and making sure she was okay.

She had to be okay.

As he approached the door, Harvey came outside.

"Hey, have you seen Bree?" Scott asked.

"Not since yesterday, why?"

The sound of a woman's scream echoed across the property.

ELEVEN

Chills shot down Scott's spine.

"Help, somebody help me!" Breanna cried.

"The barn!" Harvey said.

Scott took off in a full-blown sprint.

"Wait," Harvey said.

Scott wasn't waiting for Harvey or anyone else. With every pump of his arms, Scott's bullet wound ached.

His heart ached more. He did this. He put Bree in the line of fire.

He got to the barn and slid into the doorway. "Breanna!"

"Up here!"

He snapped his attention toward the second level storage area but didn't see her. Did her attacker have her pinned up there behind the stacks of boxes ?

Harvey came up beside him. "Where is she?"

"Up there. Let her go!" Scott ordered.

"I can't let go, I'm stuck!" Bree called down to them.

Scott and Harvey rushed to the far side of the barn and looked up. She was hanging from the ceiling by her ankle.

"How did you—"

"Please get me down," she interrupted Harvey.

Concerned, yet relieved, Scott finally took a breath. She had a mishap, an accident. No one was threatening her with a gun. They hadn't followed through on their threat. Yet.

Scott studied the rope attached to her leg and noticed the other end tied around a cast iron decorative fountain.

"Come on," he said to Harvey.

Scott went to the fountain to untie the rope.

"Here." Harvey pulled out a knife.

"No, then you won't be able to lower her down easy," Scott said. "By untying it we've got all this slack to work with."

"Thanks for not taking any pictures," Bree joked.

Scott looked up at her in question.

"Ya' know, to totally embarrass me on Facebook."

She was being awfully calm considering her position dangling upside down like a turkey ready to be plucked. Then again, maybe the lightheartedness was a cover for the fear that had to be coursing through her body.

It must be terrifying to be strung up in such a vulnerable way. Scott couldn't help but wonder if this was a mere accident or if it was a calculated threat to drive home the caller's message.

Figure it out or we'll end that pretty blonde nurse of yours.

"Almost done," Scott said, loosening the knot. "Harvey, grab hold of the rope and we'll let her down easy."

"Try not to drop me on my head," Bree said.

Harvey grabbed the rope and Scott completely loosened the knot, reaching the rope, as well.

"I can manage her weight," Harvey said. "You get beneath her and cushion her landing."

"My landing? Oh, boy," Bree said.

Scott nodded at Harvey and let go. The older man had a solid grip of the rope and didn't seem to strain against Bree's weight.

Although why would he? The petite Bree probably didn't weight much more than a hundred pounds.

"Okay, nice and easy." Scott positioned himself beneath her. Keeping eye contact, he forced a gentle smile to let her know everything was going to be okay.

She jerked down a few inches and flailed her arms. "Yikes!"

"Sorry," Harvey said. "It's like driving a new car. Have to get used to the brakes."

As Harvey lowered her a little more, Scott could tell her eyes were watering. The pain must be worse than she let on. Or was it the fear?

"A little faster." Scott reached out to catch her.

"Yep," Harvey said.

He lowered her in jerky movements, probably trying to balance her weight against his own, until she was only inches from Scott's outstretched arms.

"Catch me," she whispered.

"You know I will," Scott said.

Another jerk and Scott got a hold of her shoulders. He turned her so she was facing him and as her tethered leg lowered to the ground, he pulled her firmly against his chest.

"Okay, I got her," Scott said.

Harvey released the rope. Scott slid his good arm beneath her knees and scooped her up. She wrapped her arms around his neck, burying her face against his shoulder.

"Go ahead and cut the rope off her ankle," Scott said.

"Yep." Harvey cut the rope.

With a shudder, Bree leaned back and looked into Scott's eyes. A part of him never wanted to let her go.

"Thanks," she said.

Scott kneeled and lowered her onto an overturned crate. "Tell me what happened." He didn't let go of her hand.

"I was looking for replacement lightbulbs, but it's a mess back there with garland and lights scattered all over. Then I heard a scuffling sound and thought it was Ruby so I went to call out to her, tripped and went flying up to the rafters."

Harvey analyzed the rope he'd cut off her ankle. "Slip knot. Awfully neat, as if..." he glanced at Scott.

"Someone intended to string her up."

"Why would anyone…" She paused. "Oh."

"This was intentional? To harm Breanna?" Harvey said in a worried tone.

"Could be." Scott pulled his hand away from Bree's and stood. "A man called my room and said if I didn't give them what they wanted they'd go after Bree."

"Then give them what they want," Harvey snapped.

"Harvey," Bree said in a scolding tone.

"What? He gives them what they want and they go away." He nodded at Bree. "They'll leave you alone."

"Problem is, I think I know what they want, but haven't a clue where it is," Scott said. "I'll figure it out. Harvey, you take care of Bree."

"Where are you going?" Bree said, rubbing her ankle.

"I have to leave."

"You mean run away?"

"I mean leave this resort, and you, behind. That way—"

"No." Bree stood and wavered.

When Scott offered his hand to steady her, she pulled away to prove she didn't need his help.

"It won't matter, Scott," she said. "They already have me on their radar. If you're here or not here, I'm still a target."

"Because of me. And that drives me crazy," he said.

She gripped his jacket and looked up into his eyes. "Then fix it. End this thing before something even worse happens."

"But—"

"They're bullies, Scott. As long as you let them stomp all over you they'll keep on stompin'. They'll threaten you and terrorize you and control your life if you let them."

From the expression in her eyes, Scott sensed she was speaking from her heart, from personal—and painful—experience.

"I want you to go away somewhere, for your own safety," he said.

"What will that prove? If they think I'm leverage over you they'll find me. I won't be safe until you find answers and we resolve this situation." She let go of his jacket and stepped around him. "Did you save me anything for lunch, because I think I've earned a turkey sandwich."

He didn't know how to respond to her casual remark. As she headed across the barn, he noticed her limping and rushed to her side.

Bree put up her hand. "Do not pick me up."

"I want to help you," Scott said.

She looked up at him with those expressive and pleading green eyes. "Then stand up to them. Fight them with everything you've got."

Bree thought she did a pretty good job of not letting on how terrified she was when she'd been strung up in the barn; but she guessed Scott knew the truth. She didn't seem to be able to keep anything from him.

Over the course of the next few hours he was attentive to her every need, from offering aspirin for her muscle pain, to heating water for her tea. He didn't even have to ask what she needed; he did what was necessary.

Now if he'd only puzzle through this mystery and put an end to the hidden threat stalking them from the shadows.

At least he'd given up trying to get rid of her. Boy, that sounded pathetic, she thought, eyeing him as he studied the computer screen.

She wasn't leaving his side until they

made some headway on this case. The whole bully thing made her crazy in ways that left her speechless. She'd spent months after her break-up analyzing her relationship with Thomas, beating herself up for not standing firm. Whenever she noticed that same bullying behavior in someone else, her anger at the injustice would practically consume her.

That's what these men were doing to Scott. They were threatening him, this guy who was functioning with a head injury, gunshot wound and bruised ribs. She wasn't going to stand for it. No, sir.

As she sipped her tea, she wondered if Harvey had told her brother about what happened in the barn. Probably not or else Aiden would have pounded on the door two hours ago. So Harvey had kept her business private. Either that, or he hadn't run into Aiden this afternoon. Knowing Harvey, it would be a casual conversation, not a specific phone call to tattle on Bree. Harvey was cool that way.

"Bree?" Scott said, studying her.

"Yeah?"

"You okay?"

"Sure, why?"

"You looked worried."

"I was wondering what my brother will do when he finds out about the barn incident."

"You mean, besides kick me out of his resort?" he said. "I'm surprised I haven't received the bill under my door by now."

"Talk about the biggest bully of them all," she muttered.

He took her hand. "Aiden is not a bully. He's a loving brother. You're lucky to have him."

"I guess. Did you find anything in your files?"

"Yes." He released her hand and refocused on the screen. "My phone calendar was synced up to my laptop so I can see what I did the week before I came to Washington, and then once I got here. I was working security for Mr. Oppenheimer, owner of GRI, in Hawaii for a week prior to my trip. Nothing remarkable there. When I got to Washington I had an appointment with someone named C.J. the day after my plane landed."

"Was there a location?"

"Healthy Eats Restaurant. I don't remember if we actually met or not."

"Oh, the new organic place."

"I'd like to take a ride over there to see if anyone remembers me."

"I've been wanting to try their soups." She grabbed her purse and stood.

"What about the Christmas decorations?"

"Ruby's got it covered." She smiled. "Hey, let's bring something home to reheat for dinner later so you don't have to order room service."

"Sounds like a plan. But if we're going out in public I'm going to need your help." He motioned her toward the door.

"With what?"

"Your instincts. Listen to them, trust them. If something seems off or suspicious, let me know, okay?"

"Of course."

"I'm not so sure my instincts are a hundred percent."

She paused and touched his arm. "It will come back to you, your memory, your instincts."

"You always sound so confident when you say stuff like that."

"You have to have faith." She smiled and they left his room.

* * *

Bree suggested they stop at her place first to let Fiona out and throw the ball to burn off some of her pup's energy. When they got to her cottage and opened the back door, Fiona bounded outside. Bree shoved a tennis ball in the stick launcher and offered it to Scott.

"Whenever I'm in a bad mood this always helps," she said. "Well, this and baking."

Fiona rushed him as he let the ball fly.

"An important characteristic for rescue dogs is the high play factor," Bree said. "And their endurance level."

Fiona rushed back to Scott and dropped the ball at his feet, wagging her tail.

"This one can go on for hours, right baby girl?" Bree said.

Scott tossed the ball again and Fiona took off. A warm smile eased across his face. The Fiona mood enhancer was working for him, too.

Bree noted his look of abandon: he was totally lost in the moment playing with her dog. Watching Fiona chase the ball with such joy always brought a smile to Bree's face.

Scott glanced over his shoulder at Bree's home. "Why aren't your Christmas lights up?"

"Aiden's supposed to help but he's been slammed at work, plus helping Mom with some house projects."

"I could help," he offered, and glanced at her, then back at the dog, "if you want."

"That would be awesome."

A sudden image of Bree and Scott sitting by the fireplace in her living room eating freshly baked pumpkin muffins crossed her thoughts. A lovely image indeed.

"You seriously like Christmas, huh?" he said, tossing the ball again.

"What do you mean?"

"The way your face lit up just now when I said I'd help put up decorations. I'll bet you're going to send me up on the roof with boxes of lights."

"Nothing so dangerous."

His smile faded, along with their moods. The word *dangerous* yanked them back to reality. They were no longer a normal couple playing catch with her dog and making Christmas plans.

He was a man being hunted for something

he couldn't remember, and Bree was the woman determined to help him.

They played with the dog for a few more minutes, then Bree put Fiona back inside.

She locked up and they got in her SUV. The short drive to Healthy Eats started off quiet. Was Scott worrying about what he'd find out at the restaurant? She noticed he kept looking into the side view mirror.

To ease the tension she clicked on the radio to a station playing Christmas music. The sound of Bing Crosby singing "White Christmas" filled the car.

"This is a fun movie. We watch it every year," she said, casting a quick glance at Scott. "What are your family traditions for Christmas?"

"Don't have any. Mom was always working, Dad was never in the picture, I'm usually working."

"What about your sister?"

"I stop by around the holidays, but she spends Christmas with her best friend, Ashley. She has a big family with lots of kids running around, playing with their new toys. That's more fun for Em than hanging out with me."

"So what do you do on Christmas Day?"

"Relax, watch football if it's on, maybe catch a movie."

"Alone?"

"Mostly." He glanced at her. "What about you?"

"For the past five years Mom's been having an open house. She's got a big old house on twenty acres. Anyone who doesn't have family is welcome as long as they bring a side dish or dessert. Mom provides the ham, turkey and beverages."

"A lot of people show up?"

"Depends on the year. The first few years it was a dozen or so. Last year we had a full house. Aiden counted 35 people, and some stayed until midnight."

"That sounds like quite a party."

She thought about Christmas last year and how embraced she had felt, how loved, in contrast to her Christmases in the city.

"What, did someone break a lamp or something?" Scott said.

"No," she chuckled. "Why did you ask that?"

"Your smile faded."

"It was the first time in a long time that I'd

felt part of a community. Living in the city had been an isolating experience for me."

"Because of your boyfriend?"

"Pretty much. He didn't approve of me hanging out with girlfriends or coming back to visit family."

"I take it he didn't attend your family Christmas party?"

"Absolutely not, and he guilted me into skipping it one year, as well."

"The guy sounds like a jerk." He glanced at her. "Sorry."

"It's okay. He was a jerk in the end. He refused to let me break up until I convinced him I wasn't good enough for him."

"You did not," Scott said, disbelief coloring his voice.

"I did what was necessary to extricate myself from a bad situation. It wasn't pretty, but it worked." She sighed, remembering how taken she'd been with Thomas when they'd first started dating. "He wasn't always a jerk. In the beginning he was polite and sophisticated, intelligent and funny. All the things I thought were important."

"And now?"

"Now, other things are important, like

kindness and integrity. But it doesn't matter because I promised myself I wouldn't date for at least a year after that breakup. The whole experience was tough, but I came back to Echo Mountain, adopted Fiona from a SAR volunteer who had to move away and give her up. Training for SAR and going on missions distracted me from my pain."

"And how long has it been, since your breakup?"

"It's coming up on a year."

He nodded and glanced out the window.

Bree realized she hadn't even been interested in dating anyone, not even a little bit and not even the safe men her mom tried fixing her up with.

Until Scott literally fell beneath her tree.

"About this restaurant," he started, "will I have to eat kale and goji berries?"

"Sure, if you want." She winked.

"I'm more of a meat loaf kind of guy."

"I'm sure we'll find something. There it is." She pointed.

"Let's hope someone recognizes me."

She parked and they got out of the car.

The restaurant was housed in a bungalow

style building with white trim and multi-pane windows.

"I've driven by a few times but never had time to go inside," Bree said as they approached the restaurant.

The door swung open and a twenty-something young man with jet-black hair stepped outside. He glanced at Scott and froze, blocking the door.

"I don't think so."

"I'm sorry?" Scott said.

"Oh, no, not good enough." The young man pulled out his cell phone.

"Who are you calling?" Bree asked.

The kid glared at Scott. "9-1-1."

TWELVE

"There must be some mistake," Bree said.

"No mistake. I told him never to come back. This is a healthy restaurant, we offer a healthy environment as well as healthy food which means no stress, or fighting."

"Look, we need your help," Bree said, hoping to keep him from making the call. "Please? Three minutes of your time. We won't even come inside."

The young man lowered his phone. "Fine."

"Thanks." She extended her hand. "I'm Breanna McBride, my brother runs Echo Mountain Resort."

"I've heard of you guys, the McBride family."

"And you are…?"

He shook her hand. "Dylan Jones."

"Oh, you're Catherine's son? I met your mom at church a few weeks ago, but I didn't see you."

"I was at work. Hospital shift."

"Dylan, my friend Scott was in an accident and is suffering from a head injury. I'm trying to help him remember things, perhaps by recreating where he's been and who he met with. Obviously you remember him being here."

"Wait, you were the guy that was shot in the mountains?" he asked.

"Yes," Scott said.

"And now you can't remember stuff?"

"Nope."

"Maybe you're better off." Dylan crossed his arms over his chest and leaned against the building.

"Can't argue with you there," Scott said. "Judging by your behavior I have a feeling I'm not going to like what I find out."

"What happened, Dylan?" Bree asked.

"He went nuts on this other guy, grabbed him by the collar and practically threw him across the room."

Dylan's mom pushed the door open. "Dylan, what's going on?" She glanced at Bree and smiled. "Oh, hi, Breanna."

"Catherine, it's nice to see you again."

"Dylan, we're supposed to encourage patrons to come into the restaurant, not keep them out."

"This is the guy, Mom, the one that started the fight last week."

Catherine eyed Scott.

"I'm sorry if I did anything to disturb you or your patrons, ma'am," Scott said. "I wish I had an explanation, but I sustained a head injury which has caused memory loss."

Catherine glanced at Bree.

"It's true," Bree confirmed. "This is the man we rescued from the trail Sunday."

"The one who was shot?"

"Yes."

"Another reason you shouldn't let him into the restaurant," Dylan said. "What if they try shooting him in here?"

"Dylan, don't be so dramatic," his mom said. "Come get something to eat." Catherine held the door open and motioned them inside.

Bree spotted a sheriff's deputy sitting in the corner sipping coffee.

"That's my brother, Nate Walsh," Catherine said. "He stops by on break. Let me introduce you."

"He's got a gun," Dylan threatened, nodding at Scott.

Catherine shook her head. "Nate, this is Breanna McBride and her friend, Scott."

Scott offered his hand. "Scott Becket."

Nate shook Scott's hand and narrowed his eyes. "The hiker who was shot and has amnesia?"

"Wow, word gets around," Scott said.

Nate shrugged. "That was pretty big stuff for this county."

Breanna also shook hands with Deputy Nate Walsh. "So nice to meet you. We were hoping that bringing Scott back to places he'd been to before the accident might help him regain his memory."

"Oh, he was here, all right," Dylan said.

"Hey, kid, can you get me a refill?" Nate held up his empty mug.

"Sure." He sneered at Scott as he passed.

"Well, have a seat anywhere," Catherine said. "This is my slow time of the day."

"Thanks," Scott said. "I hate to press, but it would probably help if your son could give me a play-by-play of what happened when I was here last."

"I'd like to hear that, too." Nate motioned

for Scott and Bree to join him in the booth and they did. She appreciated sitting with a police officer, thinking maybe it would keep the bad guys at a distance.

"Well, I have food to prep," Catherine said with a smile. "Keep in mind, Dylan tends to embellish when he has an audience."

"So you don't think Scott got violent?" Bree said.

"I'm sure something happened, but he certainly didn't tear up the place. There was no damage to speak of. Anyway, nice to see you again, Breanna."

"Thanks, you, too."

Catherine disappeared into the kitchen as Dylan returned to the table with the pot and poured coffee for his uncle.

"So, Dylan," Nate started, "tell me again what happened when Scott here tore up the place."

Dylan set the pot on the table. "Are you messing with me?"

"No, I'd like to hear the story again. He got into a fight and what, threw chairs or something?"

Dylan sighed and nibbled at the corner of his mouth. "Not exactly."

"Okay, then what, he made a mess of the table, left you a bad tip?"

"Forget it." Dylan turned to walk away.

"Dylan, please," Scott said. "I could seriously use your help. Anything you could tell me about what I said or how I acted, or anything about the man I was talking to—"

"You weren't talking," Dylan spun around. "You were yelling. The argument started in here, then continued out in the parking lot."

"I didn't do anything violent in the restaurant?"

"You pounded on the table and spilled water everywhere."

"Ah, so you were upset that you had to clean up," his uncle said.

"You didn't see him, Uncle Nate. He looked scary." Dylan glanced at Scott. "Sorry, but you did."

"Don't be sorry. Could you give us a description of the other guy?"

"He was older." He glanced at his uncle. "Even older than you."

"Why, thanks," Nate muttered.

"He had gray in his hair and wore a leather jacket and a blue baseball cap with a red *C* on the front."

Bree gripped Scott's leg. "The man who tried to get to you in the hospital."

"And did get to me in my hotel room," Scott said. "So I knew him pretty well if we met for lunch."

"You might know him, but you didn't like him," Dylan said.

"Go on," Nate encouraged.

"When I was cleaning up your table, you guys kept talking like I was invisible. The other guy said, 'the boss says it's over, then it's over.' You said, 'I'm doing this to save the boss.' You said something about talking directly to your boss and the other guy made a snide comment as I was walking away. That's when I heard a crash and the flower vase hit the floor. When I turned around, you had him by the collar of his jacket. You were breathing fire, man, I thought you were going to strangle him, so I threatened to call 9-1-1 and you left. I watched you guys in the parking lot. He was pretty calm, but you were waving your arms, trying to make your point."

"And you'd never seen the older man before, and you haven't seen him since that day?" Deputy Nate asked.

"No, sir, I'd remember. He was one creepy-looking dude."

"Thanks, Dylan. You've been a big help," Scott said.

Bree puzzled over the conversation Dylan just shared.

"You guys want coffee? It's organic, fair trade," Dylan offered to Scott and Bree.

"Sure, I'll have a cup," Scott said.

"Do you have any tea?" Bree asked.

"I'll bring over the list. It's also organic and loose leaf."

"Sounds great."

Dylan left the table.

"Does that help?" Nate asked.

Scott nodded. "It confirms that I was here for work on a special project for my boss."

"Then why would your boss send the salt-and-pepper haired man to stop you?" Bree asked.

"Maybe he didn't. Maybe Rich was lying."

They three of them sat quietly for a few seconds.

"Well, I'd better get back." Deputy Nate shifted out of the booth. "Watch yourselves and let me know if I can help with anything."

He jotted his cell number on a —restaurant business card and slid it across the table.

"Thanks," Scott said.

Dylan returned, offered Bree a tea list and poured Scott a cup of coffee.

"Oh, there was one other thing," Dylan offered.

"What's that?" Scott said.

"You asked if I knew where the refinery plant was in Wallace County. You said something about your GPS not being able to find it or something."

"And did you give me directions?"

"I did. Are you guys ordering food? We have a tasty butternut squash soup that's dairy and gluten free."

"I'll have the paradise green tea but could you give us a few minutes on our food order?" Bree said.

"Absolutely."

Dylan went into the back and Bree placed her hand over Scott's. "This helps, right? Now you know you were headed to the plant."

"I need to get up there."

"It'll be dark in a few hours. Let's go tomorrow."

He looked into her eyes. "I'd rather you stay at the resort."

"And hide? No, thanks. If these jerks are after me, too, then I'd like to be a part of the investigation. Besides, I'm with you until the end of this thing."

"Bree—"

"If you're worried about our safety, we could get one of the SAR guys to come with us, or better yet I'll ask Uncle Chuck to meet us there. It's in his county."

"A cop," he hedged. "I don't know what I'm going to find up there."

"You mean something that will reflect poorly on you?"

"You have such a nice way of saying things. Yes, I'm afraid I've participated in something criminal and it'll come out if I keep pushing."

"I doubt it, but facing your mistakes is the only way to move on with your life or they will shadow you forever."

He cocked his head slightly and a tender smile tugged at his lips. "How did you get so wise?"

"I've had my share of challenges," she said, "but in the end they made me stronger."

"You're amazing."

The words sent a shiver across her shoulders. Thomas used to call her that. Bree leaned back and studied him. Scott wasn't working an angle to get something in return. He sincerely meant it. He considered her an amazing individual.

"Uh, the brain injury has kind of messed with my filter, so was that one of those things I should have kept to myself?" he asked.

"No, actually, I'm glad you didn't."

The next morning Bree got up early and did a majority of her resort work so she could take a long lunch and drive Scott to the plant. She called Uncle Chuck who agreed to meet them, so everything was all set. Since Aiden had business in Seattle he wasn't around to hammer her with twenty questions when she left the resort with Scott.

As they headed north in her SUV she noted that Scott was unusually quiet. "How's your head?" she asked.

"Better than yesterday."

"That's good."

A few minutes of silence stretched between them.

"Are you okay?" she asked.

He glanced at her. "What do you mean?"

"You seem...distant."

"I'm focused on making sure we're not being followed," he said, squinting as he studied the side view mirror.

"How does it look?"

"Good."

Another few minutes of silence. Bree assumed Scott was anticipating the worst; that he wouldn't like what he discovered at the plant.

"It will be okay," she offered.

He nodded and glanced out the window.

"Okay, spill it."

He snapped his attention to her. "What?"

"Whatever's bothering you. I have to know because it's driving me nuts and I'm making up stories in my head."

"Stories?"

"Yes, like you don't want me around, or you remembered something terrible, or—"

"I want you around." He glanced back out the window. "I want this whole thing over."

"It will be. You have to have faith."

"I wish I knew how to do that."

"Just ask."

He frowned at her in question.

"Close your eyes and ask God for guidance in helping you navigate through this challenge."

"I have no right to—"

"You do, Scott. We all do."

With a sigh he closed his eyes for a few seconds, and when he opened them he seemed better, less tense. They still didn't speak much during the ride up to the plant, but she didn't push it.

Thirty minutes later they pulled into a long driveway that led to a large parking lot. There were only a few cars scattered throughout the lot, which seemed odd.

"It's the middle of the workday. Shouldn't there be more cars?" she said.

"You would think."

"There's my uncle's cruiser." She found a spot nearby, but Uncle Chuck wasn't in the car. "Maybe he's already inside."

They shared a concerned look, then got out of the car. As she stepped up to Scott he put out his hand. "Stay behind me."

"Okay."

She appreciated that he was being cautious, but she wasn't too worried since her uncle was here. They approached the main door.

"There's got to be an intercom or something to let them know we're here."

Bree observed that the door was ajar. "Scott." She nodded.

He pushed it open.

The first thing Bree noticed was how quiet it was inside the building, as if it was abandoned. "This is creepy."

Scott pointed at a sign down the hall that read Research & Development. "Let's try there first."

They went down the hall and followed the arrows. Turning the corner, she wondered if this could be considered trespassing. She also wondered what happened to Uncle Chuck. Was he inside speaking with an employee?

"What are you looking for?" she asked, placing her hand against Scott's back.

He pushed open the double doors and froze. "This."

Bree glanced around him into the room.

There was nothing there, no research equipment, computers or even furniture.

"Did they close the plant?" she said.

"Not that I know of."

They wandered around the room looking for something, anything to help make sense of the situation.

"It's almost like it never existed," she said.

"Or everything was destroyed."

"By whom?" she said.

He shook his head. "No clue."

"We should find my uncle."

Scott took her hand and led her out of the empty research room. As they headed back to the main office, Bree peered through office windows as they passed. Desks and bookshelves were empty—no computers, books or supplies. The place was definitely closed for business.

"Hang on." Scott paused beside a set of double doors.

The sign above read Assembly.

He pushed open the doors and they entered a huge room with high ceilings, cement walls and no windows. Twenty-foot metal racks were lined up in rows.

"Where is everything?" he said.

"What should be in here?"

"According to the website, portable refinery containers and braces to hold them in place while the chemical is infused into the containers."

"Maybe they've been shipped out?"

"There'd still be equipment to assemble the product," he said.

Something sparkly caught Bree's attention on the floor. She bent down to pick it up.

A shot rang out.

She instinctively stayed down. Scott dropped to the floor and got in her face. "Stay here," he ordered, shifting her further behind the metal rack.

"Don't—"

He stopped her protest with a kiss. His lips were warm and soft, and she was so shocked by the tender and loving gesture that she couldn't speak when he broke the kiss and took off. Scott darted down the side of the wall, using the metal racks as cover. She guessed he was going after the shooter.

She slipped out her cell phone to call 9-1-1, but realized it would take them too long to get here. She decided to call her uncle instead.

Two more shots rang out. Biting back a shriek, she eyed her phone and willed her trembling fingers to press the right buttons.

Another shot rang out.

Her eyes watered with fear. If anything happened to Scott after everything he'd been through...

She searched her phone's address book for her uncle's number.

A crash bounced off the ceiling and the sound of grunting men echoed through the room. She eyed the door. To get there, to escape, she'd have to expose herself to the gunman.

Bree stuck with plan A and dialed her uncle's number.

Another shot rang out.

Then silence.

She hit Send on her phone.

And the sound of Uncle Chuck's cell phone rang across the room.

THIRTEEN

By the time Scott got to Bree's uncle he was down on the cement floor, gripping his shoulder. Scott pulled him behind the metal rack.

"Go, go protect Bree," Chuck said.

"You're coming with me."

"I'll slow you down."

"Make sure you don't."

Uncle Chuck glared at Scott and Scott glared back, challenging the older man to reach deep down and find the strength to get up.

"Where is she?" Chuck asked.

"Down there by the door. Ready?"

Chuck nodded, his expression unsure.

"On three. One, two, three." Scott shielded Chuck against the wall and they jogged toward Bree's hiding spot.

Scott couldn't move fast enough, but the

pain from Chuck's wound was obviously slowing him down. A shot pinged above Scott's head. It wasn't easy hitting a target shielded by metal racks. From this angle, Scott had a pretty good guess where the shooter was positioned.

Scott would get Uncle Chuck and Bree safely to her car; then he'd conceal himself and wait for the guy to leave. Scott wasn't looking for trouble, but this guy was his best lead to figuring out why he had come to Echo County in the first place.

When they got close to Bree, a knot formed in Scott's throat. She was huddled like a little girl afraid of a monster in her bedroom closet.

"Bree, it's okay," Scott said, kneeling beside her. She glanced at him with those big green eyes. "Come on." He helped her up. She noticed Uncle Chuck's bloody hand gripping his arm.

"Uncle Chuck," she gasped.

"I'll be fine once I get you out of here."

A bullet hit the cement wall above them and Bree yelped as they all took cover.

"New plan," Scott said to Uncle Chuck. "I'll draw his fire and you get her out of here."

"Scott, no," she said.

Scott ignored her and nodded at her uncle.

"Let me call it in first." Chuck grabbed the radio on his shoulder and called in the code for shots fired and officer down. That would get local cops and state troopers racing to the scene.

Another shot echoed through the assembly room and Bree leaned against Scott's chest. He gave her a solid hug, waiting until her uncle was ready to make a run for it.

"Why don't we wait for the police?" her muffled voice said against Scott's jacket.

"It'll take too long. Get ready to run."

"I won't abandon you," she said with a tight jaw.

"This isn't your decision to make," Scott said. He released her and shoved her at her uncle. "If anything happened to you I'd never forgive myself. If you care about me, you won't do that to me."

Her expression softened. "Be careful."

Uncle Chuck grabbed her arm and leaned in the direction of the door. He nodded at Scott. "Whenever you're ready."

Scott took a deep breath, peered around the metal shelves he was using as cover, and took off. He'd had experience outmaneuvering the enemy but this was different. There was more than just his life at stake; Bree's life was at stake, as well.

A bullet pinged the metal behind him, but didn't ricochet and clip Scott. He swerved one way, then the other, focused on the exit, not the marksman. No use letting that image mess with his head: Scott as a duck in a carnival shooting gallery.

He was almost to the door when the shooting stopped. He sprinted outside, finding a spot behind a cluster of trees to wait for the shooter to exit. Struggling against the adrenaline rush, he planned his next move: getting to the shooter without being shot himself.

But the shooter didn't leave the building, at least not through any door that Scott could see. Had he followed Bree and her uncle out front?

"No," he ground out and took off around the perimeter of the plant. When he got to the front, Bree's car was gone.

A door slammed. Scott jerked his head around and saw a short, stocky guy running for a black sedan—the same car that had tried to pick up Bree the other day.

The shooter must have emptied his clip and was fleeing the premises.

Scott charged the guy, tackling him before he could get to his car.

"Why are you shooting at me?" Scott demanded.

"Because I'm bored." The guy struggled against the hold.

"Tell me!"

Instead, he slugged Scott in the stomach.

Scott's grip loosened.

Stocky guy pummeled Scott in the arm where he'd been shot. Scott fought to keep a tight hold, but the guy flipped Scott over and they rolled, Scott fighting the burn of his gunshot wound. He threw a few punches and hit his mark, but was at a disadvantage thanks to his previous injuries.

The shooter nailed Scott in the jaw and he saw stars, but managed to stay conscious. He had to restrain the guy, get him to talk. Scott broke free and reached for a nearby rock to use as a weapon.

Three shots rang out.

Scott hit the ground and scrambled behind a car in the lot.

His arm burned and his jaw ached but it

was nothing compared to the fear flooding through his body. Did the guy have an accomplice?

"Scott!" Breanna's voice cried out.

He fisted his hand and slammed it into the quarter panel of the car. Not only did the guy have an accomplice, but he'd also gotten his hands on Bree.

Scott had no choice but to sacrifice himself for Bree's safety. He needed to convince them to let her go.

With a deep breath, he stood and raised his hands in surrender.

Instead of seeing Bree restrained by a heartless thug, she was running in Scott's direction. Confused, he slowly lowered his hands and spotted the stocky guy sprawled on the ground, blood staining his jacket. In the distance Uncle Chuck clutched his gun, looking a little stunned. Scott wondered if the guy had ever killed a man.

Reality struck hard: if the guy was dead, so was Scott's best lead.

He caught Bree as she launched herself into his arms. "I told you to get out of here," he said.

"Lecture me later. I'm so glad you're okay."

Only then did he realize she was trembling. He held her tight and stroked her hair. "Shh, it's okay."

Scott would have been a lot better if he could have forced information out of the guy lying on the ground.

Chuck went to the body, pressed his fingers against the man's throat and glanced at Scott. "He's gone."

Bree glanced down at the body. "That's the guy who tried to pick me up outside the police station."

Scott turned her away from the dead body.

Sirens echoed in the distance.

"I had no choice." Uncle Chuck stood, looking a little pale.

Scott released Bree. "Hang on, buddy." Scott went to steady Chuck, who started to waver on his feet. "Let's find you a place to sit down."

As Scott and Bree led Chuck to a nearby picnic bench a man came out of the plant. He was in his forties, wore a uniform and winced as he pressed his hand against the back of his head.

"Who are you?" the guy asked.

"Scott Becket, this is Breanna McBride

and Police Chief Trainer." Chuck sat down with a dazed expression.

The uniformed guy joined them. "Police chief?"

"Of Wallace Falls," Chuck said. "And you are?"

"Pete Baker, security guard."

"Where were you when all this was going on, Pete?" Scott challenged.

"Inside. Some guy nailed me in the back of the head and I was out." He glanced at the stocky guy, then back at Scott. "What's going on here?"

"It's a long story," Scott said.

"Scott lost his memory and is trying to get it back," Bree said as she pressed her scarf against her uncle's wound. "Someone told us Scott had been up here so we came to check it out, maybe jar something loose. Do you remember meeting Scott?"

It struck Scott how incredibly trusting she was, and focused. She'd seen a man shot down in front of her but was still on task: she wanted to help Scott remember.

Pete studied Scott. "No, I can't say we've met, but there are five other security guards who work twelve-hour shifts."

"When did the plant close?" Scott asked.

"I'm not sure. I came on board a few weeks ago and the place was already empty."

"Then why hire you?" Bree asked.

"Vandalism," Chuck chimed in. "Bored teenagers get into mischief."

"So far only broken windows." Pete hesitated and glanced at Chuck, then at the stocky guy. "Until today."

"I told you not to hang out with this guy, he's trouble," Chuck scolded Bree.

"Don't get snappy. I'm not the one who shot you, Uncle Chuck. And Scott saved your life back there," she countered.

Pete eyed them with curiosity.

"Sorry, family spat," she said.

Two squad cars headed in their direction, followed by an ambulance.

Scott took his last chance to get information before local law enforcement shut him out. "You have no idea why the plant closed down?" he asked Pete.

"None."

"Who do you report to? Is he onsite?" Scott pressed.

"No, sir. I work for Magnum Security Service. Companies contract with us for jobs like this all over the country."

Scott glanced at the plant. "Another dead end."

"Hey." Bree touched his arm. "This eliminates one thing off the list and puts us that much closer to the answer."

Bree wasn't going to let Scott drift into that sinkhole of despondence. She knew depression could be a side effect of a brain injury. She'd been there herself once, depressed and pulled down into the darkest corner of her mind, feeling as though nothing would ever work out again.

After being questioned by the local authorities, Bree and Scott were released and stopped by the E.R. to check on Uncle Chuck. He must have called Bree's mom because she was at the hospital by the time she and Scott arrived.

"Oh, honey," Mom said, giving Bree a hug.

"I'm okay." She broke the embrace. "How's Uncle Chuck?"

"He'll be okay. It was a through-and-through." Mom glanced at Scott. "How are you, young man?"

"Fine, thank you."

"You don't look fine." She nodded at his arm. Blood was seeping through his shirt-sleeve.

"Come on, let's get that looked at." Bree started to lead him toward the registration desk.

"I can manage. You stay with your mom."

Bree sighed. "I'll be right here."

Scott offered a pained smile and walked away.

"Should I be worried?" Mom said.

"He probably pulled a few stitches," Bree said, watching him disappear around the corner.

Mom touched Bree's shoulder. "I meant, should I be worried about you?"

"No, why? I'm fine. We're all fine."

Mom led Bree to the waiting area and motioned for her to sit down. Bree didn't like what was coming next, undoubtedly a lecture.

"What were you doing up there at the plant?" Mom asked.

"Helping Scott check something out."

"And someone shot at you?"

"Mom—"

"You could have been seriously hurt."

"I wasn't. Uncle Chuck and Scott were there to protect me."

"You wouldn't have needed protection if you weren't trying to help Scott," she countered.

"What was I supposed to do? The guy needs to figure out his life. He doesn't have a car or—"

"He's an adult. He can rent a car," she said. "I think it's something else. I think you're falling for this man."

Bree studied her fingers. *Busted.*

"It doesn't matter," Bree said. "Once he resolves his situation he'll head back to Chicago and I'll never see him again."

"Oh, honey, then why put yourself in emotional and physical danger for him?"

Bree looked into her mother's eyes. "Because he's a good man and I haven't known many of those."

Mom placed her hand over Bree's. "Sweetie, don't let—"

"He needs my help, Mom," Bree said. "I can't turn my back on him."

Bree and Scott returned to the resort around dinnertime. She suggested they order room service, but he said he wanted to sleep and would order it later.

He was dismissing her for the evening, at least that's how it felt. So she went back to her place and straightened up, then took Fiona for a walk on the resort property. She kept Scott's room in her sights as she passed by. A soft glow emanated from behind the sheer curtains. Figuring he was awake, she considered swinging by, but stopped herself. She didn't want to seem desperate, because she wasn't.

He'd been clear that he wanted some space, the night to recover from the day's events. She couldn't blame him.

The resort's Christmas lights clicked on, bathing her in a soft glow of green, red and white.

"Look at that, Fiona," she said. "It's almost Christmas."

"What are you doing out here?" Aiden said, locking the barn and heading toward her.

"What does it look like?" *Ease up, Bree. He's your brother and he loves you.* "Fiona needed a walk. The lights look great."

"Think we need more?" he asked.

Awesome, they were talking about work, having a normal conversation.

"More? Hmm. I think the split rail is perfect, but—" Bree turned and studied the building "—maybe more on the lodge itself?"

"I purposely didn't put a lot up there because the guests can't see it from their windows."

"Yes, but think about how it will look if they take a walk, or even how pretty it would look to frame the outline of the building with a row of icicle lights in front."

"Huh, now there's an idea. I don't suppose you'd want to climb up there and string them along the roof?"

"Not in my job description." She winked.

"Speaking of your job, I heard you took off early to help that guy."

"Scott."

"Whatever. Mom called."

"And we were having such a nice conversation about Christmas lights," Bree muttered.

"I've given up on the lectures."

She smiled at him. "Really?"

"Don't look so pleased. I'm still your boss and you still owe me thirty hours a week."

"I know that, Aiden."

"Good. I'll walk you back to the cottage."

Bree wasn't going to win an argument about wanting to stay out a little longer. Aiden obviously had things to do, but he wouldn't leave her until he knew she was safely home.

Her brother needed a distraction, and not a business distraction. She'd told her friend Billie she planned to play matchmaker with Aiden, only she hadn't found the perfect woman to counter Aiden's strength and obstinate nature.

She'd worry about that later, after Scott's situation was resolved.

"Thanks," she said to Aiden as she approached her porch. She motioned Fiona into the yard and shut the gate. No reason the dog couldn't enjoy another hour of fresh air.

"Be good," Aiden said in that brotherly tone.

"Of course." She went inside.

Locking the door behind her, she realized how much she craved Christmas in her own home. She decided to pull a few things out of her storage closet to get in the spirit of Christmas. Tonight she'd check strands of lights to make sure there weren't any burned out bulbs and who knows, maybe she'd hang some tomorrow. With all the craziness going on, it would be nice to focus on something normal.

Heading for the kitchen, she heard Fiona burst into a round of aggressive barking outside. Must be a bear, or coyote. She went to the sink to pour a glass of water.

And noticed a strange car out back.

Shivers trickled across her back. *Listen to your fear; respect it.* The most important lesson she'd learned in self-defense class.

The floorboards creaked behind her.

A man was in the room.

Focus and visualize your next move. Do not let him sense your fear.

"You need to come with me," a deep male voice said.

She took a slow, calming breath.

"If you come willingly, everything will be okay."

"Who are you?" she said, readying herself for battle.

"I'm a problem solver. Becket's a problem and you can help me solve it."

He touched her shoulder.

She spun around and delivered a palm strike to the nose to disorient him.

"Ah!" The guy instinctively reached for his nose.

She went on the offensive, delivering three quick punches. He gasped and stumbled back.

Bree took off for the front door. Her phone, where was her phone? Racing through the cottage, her heartbeat pounding in her ears, she rushed down the front steps and glanced briefly over her shoulder—

And slammed into another man's chest.

FOURTEEN

"No!" she cried, her eyes pinched shut as she struggled to get away. She would not be brutalized by these men, not in front of her home with her dog on the other side of the fence, and her brother a few hundred feet away.

She slammed her boot against the top of his foot.

"Ouch, Breanna, stop. It's me."

She opened her eyes and was looking up at Scott.

"A man," she gasped, gripping his jacket. "There's a man in my house."

"Get Fiona and go get security."

Adrenaline clouding her thoughts, she didn't move for a second.

"Come on." He led her to the fence and opened the gate. Fiona barked and danced around him. "I know, girl, I know," he said, petting her head. "Go to the resort and find security, now!"

Bree took off, commanding Fiona to pace beside her. They sprinted across the property, Bree panicked not only about her own safety, but also Scott's. She needed to get help, and fast.

She swiped her key card and rushed into the southeast entrance. Grabbing the nearest wall phone, she dialed the security office. No one answered.

She rushed to the front desk, Fiona obediently sticking close, and spotted Nia working on a computer. "Nia, find Harvey, or Aiden, or both."

"What's going on?" Nia pressed buttons on her phone and held the receiver to her ear.

"Someone broke into my place."

Nia refocused on the phone. "Harvey, it's Nia. Someone broke into Bree's cottage.... No, she's here with me."

"Scott's over there," Bree offered.

"Scott Becket is at Bree's—"

"What was he doing there?" Aiden's angry voice said as he approached.

Bree whirled around. "I don't know. I went inside after you left and there was a guy in my kitchen and he said he's a problem solver and Scott's the problem, but I'm the solution and…and…"

"Whoa, take a breath." Her brother pulled her into a hug. "You're okay now."

She pushed against his chest. "Yes, but no, but Scott went inside to check it out and he could be in trouble. You've got to help him, Aiden."

Aiden glanced calmly at Nia. "Where's Harvey?"

"On his way to the cottage."

"Good. Call 9-1-1."

"Yes, sir."

Aiden looked at Bree. "It's handled, okay?"

It wouldn't be okay until she knew Scott was safe. She also knew her brother had combat training and could help Harvey neutralize a dangerous man.

"You have to help them, Aiden."

"Bree—"

"Why won't you help, because it's Scott and you don't care if he gets hurt? How can you be so selfish?"

"You are my priority, Bree, not some stranger who keeps putting you in danger," Aiden said.

"Coward."

Nia gasped. Bree regretted the word the minute it came out of her mouth, but she couldn't control her frustration.

Aiden held her gaze, his bright blue eyes filled with what seemed like shame.

"I'm sorry," Bree said. "I'm upset, please forgive me."

"If you promise to stay here, I'll go help Harvey."

Bree studied him, trying to figure out what was going on inside that head of his.

"I'm waiting," he said.

"I promise."

He nodded at Nia. "Keep an eye on my sister."

"Yes, sir."

Aiden marched down the hall, ripping the radio off his belt. Fiona started to follow him.

"Fiona, right here," Bree said.

The retriever rushed back to her master.

"I shouldn't have said that," Bree whispered.

"No kidding," Nia muttered.

Bree snapped her attention to the twenty-six-year-old concierge. "I'm worried about

Scott," Bree said, "and Aiden was an Army Ranger so why wouldn't he offer to help? I mean, what am I missing?"

Nia fiddled with the computer. "Let's see, he was an Army Ranger and now in civilian life he avoids violent situations." Nia glanced up at Bree. "You do the math."

"Wait, you mean he's having PTSD issues?"

Nia nodded.

"How could I not know this? And how did you know?"

Nia shook her head.

"Nia? Tell me."

"A couple of months ago I came in early to work out before my shift and was doing a few laps around the property. I heard a man shouting, a frightening sound. It was coming from Aiden's cottage. His bedroom window was open so I peeked inside." She sighed. "He was having a nightmare. It was horrible."

"What did you do?"

"I pounded on the front door to wake him up. When he finally made it to the door, he looked confused and disoriented. I realized I didn't have a valid reason for knocking."

"His nightmare."

"I didn't want him to know that I'd heard him, so I made something up about the chocolate tour in Seattle for our guests."

Bree glanced down the hall where Aiden disappeared. "You think violence triggers the nightmares?"

"It's a logical assumption."

"He should talk to someone, Reverend Charles, or a counselor."

"Your brother is a proud man. That would be admitting he has a problem."

"No wonder he dislikes Scott."

"What do you mean?" Nia asked.

"Scott represents violence and vulnerability."

"A traumatic combination."

A police cruiser pulled up in front of the resort, lights flashing, but no siren.

Officer Carrington rushed into the lobby. "There was a call for breaking and entering?"

"Yes, my cottage. Come on, this is the quickest way."

"Bree, you promised to stay here," Nia said.

"I'll keep my distance, promise."

Bree motioned to the cop and they headed down the hall and out the back. In the distance, Bree could make out the silhouette of Harvey's security truck, but not much else.

"Is the intruder still on the premises?" Officer Carrington asked.

"I don't know, but I think Scott went inside to check it out and Harvey and my brother went to help him."

"Wait here."

She watched him jog across the property and approach her cottage, withdrawing his firearm. As Fiona danced around her legs, Bree kept her eyes trained to her house. She wanted to go there so badly, but wouldn't break her word to Aiden, especially after realizing what he was risking by being there.

Please, Lord, don't let the intruder hurt Scott or cause my brother any more emotional pain.

Understanding her brother's condition helped Bree make sense of his behavior this past week. It also flooded her with compassion that countered her frustration with his overprotectiveness.

The minutes passed slowly, Fiona anxious to either go for a walk or go home, and Bree anxious to know if the three men she cared about were safe.

Someone got in the truck and it headed toward her. Harvey pulled into a nearby parking spot. She rushed to the driver's side window.

"It's okay, he's gone," Harvey said. "I think Officer Carrington is going to want a description from you."

"Aiden?"

"He's still there, told me to find you and bring you back."

"And Scott?"

"By the time he got into the house the guy was gone."

She and Fiona climbed into the front seat for the short drive.

"I'm sorry," Harvey said.

"What? Why?"

"I should have told your brother about you hanging from the rafters, but I didn't want to put one more thing on his plate. I should have known they'd come after you in your own place."

"Don't be ridiculous. The only people to blame here are the men after Scott."

They pulled up in front of her cottage and got out. Aiden was waiting on the front porch.

"Your friend is fine," Aiden said.

"Thank you so much." She went up and gave him a hug.

"Pack a bag."

"Why?" she said.

"I want to move you into the resort where you'll be safe."

"No."

"What are you trying to prove here, Bree?"

Scott stepped out onto the porch and she hugged him, as well.

"Are you okay?" she asked.

"Fine, frustrated that he got away, but fine."

"I'm so glad you were here when I came running outside." She broke the embrace and looked at him. "Why were you here?"

"I wanted to apologize for sending you away earlier. I was a little harsh."

"Like that's ever worked with my sister," Aiden muttered.

"She's not buying your idea about moving into the resort?" Scott said.

Aiden shook his head.

Scott tipped her chin with his forefinger so she'd look into his eyes. "We want you to be safe. There's better security at the lodge and—"

"I won't be bullied out of my own home."

"Then you need tighter security," Aiden said. "I'll call Quinn and get his approval to install a foolproof security system tomorrow."

"Until it's up and running, I'm not leaving your side," Scott said.

"If anyone's staying close, it's me," Aiden countered.

"Let's make it three and have a slumber party." Harvey marched up the stairs into the house and Fiona enthusiastically followed him.

"Wait, wait, wait," Bree said. "I don't need all of you here."

"Yeah, well—" Aiden walked up to her and hesitated "—maybe we need to be here." He disappeared into the house.

"Come on, let's get you inside," Scott said,

scanning the property. "Officer Carrington is still going through the house, but he'll take your statement when he's done."

"It was the salt-and-pepper-haired guy—Rich."

They stepped into the house and Scott shut the door, took her hands and said, "I am truly sorry for any pain I've caused you."

"It's not your fault, but thanks."

The next morning Scott awoke to the smell of cinnamon and nutmeg. He stretched and opened his eyes.

And saw Aiden glaring down at him holding a cup of coffee.

"Morning, sunshine," Aiden said.

"Yep" is all Scott could get out. He was still a little groggy from his awkward night's sleep on the living-room sofa. Aiden took the second bedroom upstairs and Harvey slept in the recliner.

"Security company is sending someone to install the alarm system today," Aiden said and sipped his coffee.

"That was fast." Scott sat up, gripping his head. The headache was back.

"Coffee might clear up that head of yours, especially Bree's coffee," Aiden said.

"Is she baking?"

"Very astute. Yes, she bakes when she's anxious. We can always tell when she's having a bad day because she comes into work the next day with plates of sweets."

"Today's gonna be one of those days, huh?" Scott rubbed his temples.

"Looks like. Come on, you look like you need a strong cup a joe."

Scott stood up, thankful that he wasn't dizzy and the bruised ribs didn't hurt too much. He had to stay sharp, had to make sure "Rich" didn't get to Bree again.

Scott followed Aiden into the kitchen and hesitated in the doorway. Not only was every counter filled with cookies, brownies, muffins and small cakes, but Bree was nowhere in sight.

"Where's your sister?" he asked.

"Upstairs changing. Guess baking is a dirty business."

"Huh."

Scott poured himself coffee and sipped. The brew tasted delicious, with a hint of something that tickled his tongue.

"Wow," he said, eyeing the mug.

"She's got many hidden talents." Aiden put his mug in the sink. "Anyway, I've got a meeting. She should be down shortly." Aiden started for the door.

"Hey, Aiden?"

"Yep?"

"Thanks for letting me stay."

Aiden glanced at Scott with more of a pleading expression than an angry one. "Figure this thing out so she's safe, okay?"

"That's the plan."

With a nod, Aiden headed down the hall to the front door.

"Hey, you're not leaving without a hug." Bree's voice carried from the top of the stairs. "Thanks again."

"Security company is coming between ten and two," Aiden said.

"But work—"

"Forget about work until this thing is over. I can't have you wandering the grounds, making yourself a target."

"But my thirty hours—"

"Take time for yourself, Bree. Consider it your Christmas bonus, okay?"

"Thanks, big brother."

Scott heard the front door shut with a click, then Bree's footsteps come down the hall. She stepped into the kitchen and froze at the sight of him.

"That bad, huh?" He fingered his hair.

"No I just… I didn't know you were awake."

She went to the stove and put on the tea-kettle.

"You're not having coffee?" he said.

"Nope, I'm a tea person, remember?"

So she'd made coffee for everyone else. That's the kind of person she was—thought-ful.

"Did you sleep okay?" she asked.

"Sure, you?"

She shrugged.

"Nightmares about last night?"

"At first." She turned. "Then I decided to change my focus and concentrate on the case. So—" she pulled a whiteboard out from behind the table "—I thought we'd play fill in the blanks."

"Board games, great," he said with teas-ing sarcasm.

"Actually, I'm hoping this game will help us figure out who's after you."

"Okay, I'm in."

* * *

Word must have gotten out about the break-in because people kept stopping by to check on Bree. A good thing since she had tons of sweets to unload from her anxiety bake-off this morning. Each time the doorbell rang she'd invite another friend into her home and serve a warm beverage with a scone or piece of sweet bread, then give them a to-go plate of muffins or cookies.

There was hardly time to focus on the whiteboard with all the people swinging by. By midmorning, Scott decided to go back to his room to change clothes.

He returned in time for lunch and she made grilled ham-and-cheese sandwiches.

"Maybe I need to put a sign on the front door," she said, as she joined him at the kitchen table.

"What kind of sign?"

"Out of Treats. That will give us a few minutes of privacy."

"Uh-oh, am I in trouble?" he teased.

"Eat your sandwich or you will be." She winked.

"You're adorable when you do that."

"Um, thanks." She took a bite of her sandwich and felt herself blush at the compliment. She wasn't used to such honesty, or admiration.

"I've been thinking...."

His eyes were locked on her and she feared blushing again since she secretly hoped he was going to say something profound about their relationship.

Instead, his gazed drifted to the whiteboard. "All roads seem to lead to one thing." He got up and with his back to her made slashing marks on the board. When he turned around, he'd drawn four different subjects in corners of the board with lines going to the center of the board and the word: *water*.

"It's all about the water samples, so let's start there. We'll make a map of all bodies of water near the plant," he said.

She grabbed her laptop off the work desk. "How many miles from the plant?"

"Make it fifty."

He leaned over her shoulder, distracting her focus. "Why don't you eat your sandwich while I do this?" she suggested.

He sat down and ate his lunch, but she felt his eyes on her.

She looked up the plant's location on the internet and used a map program to draw a fifty-mile radius around the property. "That would be Mt. Vernon to the north and Renton to the south." She turned the laptop around so he could see it. "You were out here at Echo Mountain in Woods Pass, but you wouldn't have been looking for samples there, would you?"

"Are there any bodies of water near Woods Pass?"

She scanned the area. "Doesn't look like it."

"Does any water travel through the pass?"

"Like runoff? Sure, but those won't necessarily be on a map."

"Doesn't the EPA take regular samples of water?"

"Not sure, but I have a cousin whose wife works for the EPA one county south of us. Maybe she has access to statewide information. I could call her?"

"That would be great."

"I'll have to call Mom to get her number." She nibbled her lower lip.

"And you don't want to?"

"She was upset about Chuck's injury and

then after last night's break-in—" she hesitated "—you're not her favorite person right
now."

"Understandable."

Bree pulled out her phone and made the
call, hoping Mom's frustration with Scott
wouldn't stop her from helping Bree contact
her cousin's wife.

"Hello?" she answered.

"Hey, Mom, it's Bree. How's Uncle Chuck?"

"Better. He's at home resting. And how
are you? Did they find the man who broke
into your cottage?"

"Not yet, but we're working on it." She realized her mistake too late.

"We?"

"Scott and I are trying to piece together
information that might help us figure out
why someone's after him, which is why I
called, actually. I need Vivienne's number."

"Vivienne? Why?"

"It's complicated."

"I'm a smart woman."

"We think this has something to do with
water in the area so it would be helpful to
know if there's been any water alerts or

strange substances in state water sources. I figured since she works for the EPA—"

"Hang on, I'll get my address book."

Bree gave Scott the thumbs-up sign. Mom seemed awfully supportive, considering.

Mom came back on the line and gave her Vivienne's cell phone number. "Be sure to tell her Aunt Maggie says hi."

"Will do."

"And when things calm down, bring your friend over for apple cider beef stew."

"You mean…?"

"Yes, I mean Scott. Aiden told me Scott came to your rescue last night."

"Yes, he did."

"Well, I'd like to thank him in person."

"Oh, okay."

"Love you, Breanna."

"Love you, too, Mom." Breanna ended the call and smiled at Scott. "Mom invited you to dinner."

"How did that happen?"

"Aiden told her you chased the guy off last night." She shrugged. "I'll call Vivienne."

Bree called her cousin's wife and got the scoop on water sources in the state of Washington. There weren't any reports of tainted water near Echo Mountain, but there were concerns about copper levels in water ten miles south of the plant. Bree thanked Vivienne and said she hoped to see her soon at a family event.

"Okay." Bree pointed to the computer. "Ten miles south of the plant they found odd levels of copper in the water at Lake Hawthorne."

"Odd as in dangerous?"

"Not quite. Sounds like they're going to retest in thirty days and investigate the source. A certain amount of copper comes naturally from the soil but too much can cause health problems."

The doorbell rang. "Must be the security company," she said.

"You going to give them a plate of cookies, too?" he teased.

She glanced at the kitchen counters, still half-full with pans of muffins, scones, cookies and breads. "I think I can spare some."

She snatched a plate of goodies off the counter and headed for the front door. Scott followed close behind.

"Check before you open that door," he said.

She eyed the peephole and saw a tall,

redheaded woman on the other side. Bree swung the door open. The woman glanced down at her with a snobbish expression.

"Christa?" Scott said.

"Oh, my God, Scott, you're okay." Side-stepping Bree, she threw her arms around Scott's neck.

FIFTEEN

What was she doing here? As Scott politely returned the hug, he shook his head in apology at Bree for Christa's sudden appearance and public display of affection. Christa's expensive perfume assaulted his nose, triggering a headache.

"How did you find me?" He broke the embrace.

She grabbed his face with her manicured hands and kissed him, hard, as if she were claiming him, branding him.

Letting Bree know he was taken.

Scott grabbed Christa's shoulders and broke the unwelcome lip-lock.

"Christa—"

"I was so worried about you. I called work and they said you'd disappeared from an assignment and I thought you might be having flashbacks from the Domingo case."

She glanced at Bree. "He has some emotional issues."

"I don't," he said. "I'm fine."

"That's not what I heard," Christa countered. "Someone told me you were shot. Oh, baby, where are you hurt? Let me make it better."

"Would you like some coffee or tea?" Bree interrupted in an oddly high-pitched voice.

"Espresso?" Christa said with a raised eyebrow.

"Nope, coffee, tea and sweets." Bree shoved the plate at Christa and she reeled as if Bree shoved cow dung in her face.

"I'm off carbs." She turned to Scott and blinked her false eyelashes.

What had Scott ever seen in this woman?

"Come on, babe," Christa said, taking his arm.

"I'm waiting with Bree for a security system to be installed."

"Can't someone else wait with her?"

Bree headed for the kitchen. "I'll call Harvey."

"There, see?" Christa said.

Scott might be a little messed up and confused, but he knew one thing for sure:

Christa didn't belong here, not in Bree's charming home.

"Why don't you go to the resort's restaurant and order lunch," he said. "I'll meet you there after Bree's friend shows up."

Christa stuck her lower lip out in a pout. "Baby, I just found you. I don't want to leave."

"Harvey will be here shortly. Go on. I need to talk to Bree."

"If you're not there in fifteen minutes I'm coming to get you, love." Christa gave Scott one last kiss on the lips and left.

He shut the door, remarking how bitter the kiss tasted, nothing like the kiss he'd shared with Bree yesterday at the plant.

With a deep sigh, he headed to the kitchen, wanting to talk to Bree about Christa. What would he say? He hesitated before crossing the threshold. Christa was part of his life, the real world, while Bree was... What? She was his Florence Nightingale; the woman who'd saved him both physically and emotionally during the past week. She'd been thrown into this situation and not by choice. If he hadn't fallen in her path she never would have met Scott, never would have protected him, and his actions never would have put her life at risk.

Reality struck him hard in the chest. Maybe this was the best thing for both of them, waking both him and Bree up to the fact he had another life with another woman. Maybe this would end Bree's need to continue protecting him.

When he stepped into the kitchen he found Bree bagging up more goodies for friends.

"Sorry about that," he said. "Christa can be a little overpowering."

"She was worried about you. Totally understandable." She glanced at him and frowned, then grabbed a paper napkin and wiped at the corner of his lips. She held up the napkin to reveal bright red lipstick. "So, are we done here?"

She quickly turned to pack up more baked goods. He realized she couldn't even look at him, so upset that he'd led her on when he was obviously in a committed relationship.

Yet if that were the case, why did he want to stay here and avoid seeing Christa? Something was off.

"Bree," he said.

"You don't have to wait for Harvey. I'll be fine."

"I won't leave you until I know you're safe."

"Do what you need to do, then."

As she flitted around the kitchen she began humming "Let it Snow." Was Scott making her nervous?

"Stop for a second." He touched her shoulder and she reeled back.

They looked into each other's eyes for a good ten seconds, not saying a word. He searched his mind for the right words, wanting to say something that would ease the tension but he came up empty.

Please, God, help me find the words....

Instead, the doorbell rang.

"That would be Harvey," she said, but didn't move.

"It is real," he said.

"What?"

"What I feel for you, it's real, Breanna."

"That's good to know. But your girlfriend is waiting."

As Christa picked at her green salad, she chattered on about how insanely worried she'd been when Scott didn't return her calls. He was catching about half of what she said, his attention focused out the window overlooking the grounds where employees were stringing more Christmas lights across the split rail fence.

On a normal day Bree would have been out there helping with the decorations. He could imagine her bright smile as she positioned the strands for maximum effect. She loved Christmas, a holiday Scott dreaded due to his family situation. While all the kids got new bikes, video games or baseball mitts for Christmas, Scott and Em were lucky to get one present under the tree. He'd never blamed Mom, but he'd lost faith in Santa at an early age and lost faith in God, as well.

Spending time with Bree had somehow opened his heart again to the possibility of faith and hope triumphing over desperation.

"Are you listening to a word I've said?"

He glanced at Christa. "What?"

"Let's go. This salad is subpar." She waved her hand in the air as if expecting every staff member in the restaurant to race to the table.

The server came by with the check and

she flung a credit card at the girl. Scott excused himself, saying he'd pack while she settled the bill.

He went to his room and appreciated the silence. As he packed up his things, he found a few empty plastic vials in the front pocket of a pair of jeans. Eyeing them, he had a flash of placing two vials in a padded envelope and handing it to someone.

He struggled to capture the image more clearly, trying to figure out to whom he'd given the vials and why. When nothing came, he shook his head and finished shoving his clothes into his duffel.

Glancing once around the room, his eyes caught on the table where Bree had savored her macaroni and cheese. That smile of utter contentment would haunt his thoughts, his dreams for years to come.

With a sigh, he left the room and left the essence of Breanna McBride behind. Or at least that's what he told himself.

Christa was impatiently waiting for him in the lobby. He followed her to a rented SUV and they took off, a knot balling in Scott's chest.

"I'm glad you've given up on your investigation. You're not a cop anymore. You have to stop seeing conspiracies where there are none. These kinds of things are best left to the local authorities and EPA."

"EPA?"

"Yes, you'd concocted this story that someone was sabotaging the GRI plant and toxins were getting into the local water supply. Like anyone would go to those lengths. Seriously, I think you need meds."

If he was mentally disturbed then why were men out to get him, and harm Bree? And if he walked away he'd be turning his back on the possibility of the local water supply being poisoned, of Bree and her family and friends getting sick.

"Stop the car," he said.

"What?"

"Stop!"

"What's wrong, are you feeling ill?" She pulled to the side of the road.

He got out and opened the back door, grabbing his duffel.

"Scott?"

"Go back to Chicago. I've got to finish this."

"You're not thinking straight. Where are you going?"

"Up north, near Lake Hawthorne."

"Okay, I'll drive."

"No, I need to do this by myself." And he didn't want to involve another innocent in his situation. He may not see a future with Christa, but he didn't want anything bad to happen to her.

"Scott, please get back in the car."

"I can't, Christa."

"But how will you get there?"

"I'll walk back to the resort and rent a car. I'll be fine."

"You want to get away from me that badly?" She hushed.

"I'm sorry you went to the trouble of finding me. I'll compensate you for your plane ticket, expenses, whatever."

"Don't be ridiculous."

"Goodbye, Christa."

"You mean, goodbye as in—"

"Yes."

"Oh." She sighed and glanced out the front window of her rental. "At least let me drive you back to the resort—"

"No, I need the walk." He turned and started back.

He didn't want her anywhere near the

resort, near Bree. Then again, shouldn't he stay out of Bree's life, as well?

"Hey, wait," she said, jogging up to him on high heels. "At least take some hydration with you." With a sad smile, she handed him a full bottle of water.

"Thanks and…I'm sorry."

"Me, too." She gave him an awkward hug, went back to her car and drove off.

He glanced over his shoulder and saw her car disappear down the highway.

They say brain injuries can change one's personality. Was that what was happening to Scott? Why he couldn't stand being around his girlfriend anymore?

Regardless, he knew he had to finish what he'd started and not run like a coward…like his dad.

This time he'd investigate the water issue without Bree at his side. It was the right thing to do, the best way to keep her safe and out of his dangerous business.

Scott rented a car and made good time to the river leading away from the plant to Lake Hawthorne. He wanted this to be a quick trip: get samples and head back to the resort without incident.

And once he made it back would he see Breanna? Probably not, although his heart ached for her. He couldn't remember feeling this way about a woman, especially not Christa.

With Christa out of his life he was in a position to explore his relationship with Bree.

"Not if you care about her," he muttered, turning the corner of another switchback.

At least he'd achieved his goal and got a water sample from the river leading to Lake Hawthorne. If his suspicions were correct, and the copper content was high, the Oppenheimer refinery plant was most likely the source of the toxins, which meant either one of Oppenheimer's enemies had sabotaged the plant, or employee error had caused the pollution of area water sources.

He'd take the sample to the authorities without involving Bree and putting her at risk.

A little worn out from the afternoon hike, he dug in his pack and grabbed the bottle of water Christa had given him. It had been a nice gesture considering she'd come all this way only to have Scott end their relationship. She had class, he had to give her that.

Something pricked the back of his neck—instinct. Scott eyed the valley below. Sure enough, the salt-and-pepper haired man with the blue baseball cap was headed in Scott's direction. How was that possible? Scott was sure he hadn't been followed.

Scott picked up his pace, following the trail to an overlook where he could watch his pursuer from a hidden spot. A few minutes later "Rich" headed back down. He must have lost Scott's trail and given up.

As Scott started down the trail, a gust of wind nearly took him over the edge. He struggled to keep his balance. His vision blurred and his eyes watered against the chill. Was he dehydrated? He took another swig of water.

In minutes the weather had gone from cool and sunny to cloudy with a wind that sucked the breath out of him. He'd have to take it slow. Staying close to the mountain wall, he took another step but the ground seemed to shift beneath him. Stumbling a few feet, he fought to maintain a sense of clarity, but everything seemed to blur together.

Everything but the image of a seventeen-year-old kid who popped up out of nowhere.

Miguel Domingo.

Scott stopped, unsteady on his feet.

"Miguel?"

"Why did you let me die?"

"I'm sorry, I'm sorry." Scott collapsed.

SIXTEEN

The next morning Bree went into her kitchen and scanned the packages of sweets ready to be delivered. She'd decided to wrap the rest of them in Christmas tissue and make them official presents.

She admitted to herself that she'd hoped Scott would be her Christmas blessing this year. How immature.

He was gone, there was nothing left of him except a pair of wool gloves he'd forgotten yesterday.

Her cell phone rang and her heart skipped, wanting it to be Scott, but she caught herself. He was out of her life. Forever.

She picked up her smartphone. Not recognizing the number, she decided to answer anyway. "Hello?"

"Hi, is Scott there?"

"I'm… No, who is this?"

"His sister. He said he'd be at this number for the next few days."

"Oh, hi, I'm Bree, his—" she hesitated "—friend. How are you feeling?"

"He told you about my accident?"

"Yes, and he was so worried. He wanted to rush back to Chicago but had some business he needed to resolve here in town."

"May I speak with him?"

"He's not here. His girlfriend came by yesterday and picked him up."

"Wait, Christa?" Emily asked.

"Yes."

"That's not right."

"What do you mean?"

"He told me they broke up last month."

"They didn't seem broken up when she came to my place." And kissed him and hugged him. "I wish I had Scott's cell number but he lost his phone in the fall."

"That's okay. I'm sure he'll check in soon."

Bree heard the concern in Emily's voice.

"If you talk to him, could you tell him thanks for sending Detective Joe to check on me?" Emily said.

"Sure."

"Are you...were you the woman who saved him?" Emily asked.

"Well, I didn't exactly save him, but I was on the rescue team that found him."

"It seems like you did more than that. Thanks, truly. My brother never lets anyone help him. It's nice that he's learning to rely on others for a change."

"It was my pleasure. Take care of yourself."

"You, too."

Bree hung up as Harvey came downstairs. He'd been rifling through her attic for more Christmas decorations.

"Hey!" he called as he placed a box in the hallway. "Did you see the text?"

She glanced at her phone and spotted the alert: 31 yo male hiker missing since night N of Lake Hawthorne meet at Rockland TH.

Lake Hawthorne area? Odd, since that's where she and Scott had been investigating.

"Maybe you should sit this one out considering everything that's going on," Harvey said.

Someone knocked at the door.

"Those vultures still coming by for goodies?" Harvey winked.

"It's Nia! Open up!"

Bree opened the door. "Hey, I already gave you your sweets."

"It's Scott. He's the missing hiker at Lake Hawthorne."

"No, he left for Chicago."

"He came back to the front desk yesterday afternoon, ordered a rental car and asked if I knew the quickest way to Lake Hawthorne. He made me promise not to tell you he was back."

"Why?"

"He was trying to protect you."

"This doesn't make any sense," Bree said, pacing her front hallway. She stopped short, struggling with growing panic and eyed Harvey. "We have to find him."

"I'm not sure you should—"

"Fiona knows Scott and likes him, a lot. We'll find him quicker with Fi on the team, and we can use these to entice her." She snatched Scott's gloves off the hallway table and waved them at Harvey.

"Okay." Harvey put up his hands in surrender. "Get your gear."

Five minutes later, Bree and Fiona were climbing into the front seat of Harvey's truck.

"Be careful," Nia said.

"Will do. You should probably tell Aiden—"

"He knows," Nia interrupted. "He's in the middle of a resort crisis or he'd join you on the mission. He feels horrible about not being there."

"That's silly."

"That's your brother."

"I'll call him on the way."

Bree shut the truck door and they headed for the Rockland Trailhead. She still couldn't believe Scott had taken off for Lake Hawthorne by himself. But then as his sister said, he wasn't one to ask for help.

Yet he'd been able to accept it from Bree.

Bree hoped they'd get to him quickly. She feared another trauma to the head could leave him even more messed up and confused.

Stay positive, she reminded herself.

A definite challenge because she was so worried about Scott.

The man she'd fallen in love with.

The man who could be injured or worse. No, she couldn't lose him this way.

Lose him? She didn't have him. Scott was already spoken for, committed to Christa, at least that's how it had seemed when the redhead with the bright red lipstick and fake fingernails showed up yesterday.

Scott had been on his way back to Chicago with Christa, yet returned to continue his search of mountain water sources. Why? Had he pieced together something else about the case?

Whatever the reason, Bree would rescue him again, make sure he was okay and then say her good-byes, again. Her eyes burned with unshed tears at the thought.

"I'm sure he's fine," Harvey offered.

She sighed, focusing on the mountain range in the distance.

He had to be.

Not only did Harvey partner with Bree to be her map reader, but off-duty sheriff's deputy Nate Walsh, who she'd met at Healthy Eats, also joined them. Nate was an experienced climber and would be an asset to their team, especially if they encountered gunmen in the mountains.

Multiple teams fanned out and began the search. Bree watched Fiona closely for behavioral clues, while Harvey consulted the topographical map to let Bree and Nate know what was up ahead.

A few hours later Fiona's behavior changed, and it wasn't a good sign. She started tasting the fallen brush.

"What's she doing?" Nate said.

"She's stressed," Bree answered.

"Wait, the last time she did that—"

"The victim was deceased," Bree interrupted Harvey. She didn't dare look at him for fear she'd lose it.

Although Mom might consider Uncle Chuck a parental figure for her kids, Bree always felt closer to Harvey in that way. She knew an offer of compassion on his part could make her break down.

They pressed on, Bree fighting the dread filling her chest. A few minutes later Fiona caught Scott's scent so Bree let her off leash. Fiona raced out of sight. Bree, Harvey and Nate followed her off the trail into the brush.

Harvey placed his hand gently on Bree's shoulder. "Maybe I should go first?"

Bree nodded and Harvey stepped around her. He went ahead of them, slogging over fallen branches and tree limbs. Harvey disappeared around the corner. Bree held her breath.

Fiona bolted out of the brush, practically knocking Bree over.

"What, girl? What is it?"

"Over here!" Harvey called.

Bree forged her way to Harvey and spotted Scott, dirty and disheveled, lying on the ground.

"Is he…?"

"He's alive, but unconscious. We might have to carry him out."

"I'm okay, I'm awake, I'm…" He opened his eyes. "How did I get here?"

Bree rushed to his side. "Are you hurt?"

"Breanna, what are you doing here?"

"We came to find you."

"We got an alert from Echo Mountain Rescue," Harvey said.

"Oh." Scott's brows furrowed in confusion.

She didn't like that look.

"Can you stand?" Nate said.

"I think so. Do I know you?"

"We met at the restaurant the other day."

"The restaurant," he repeated. "Right."

Scott seemed unusually disoriented. Had

he suffered another blow to the head? He managed to get up on his own but wavered, so Nate offered his shoulder for support.

"It's at least an hour hike down. Are you up to it?" Nate asked.

"Sure," Scott answered.

Nate led Scott out of the brush and back to the trail.

Scott stopped short. "What about Miguel?"

"Who?" Bree questioned.

"Miguel Domingo. He was here…." His voice trailed off as he scanned the forest. "I can't leave him here, alone."

Harvey shot Bree a look of concern.

"Scott, we need to take care of *you* right now," Bree said.

He acted as if he didn't hear her. She framed his face with her hands and turned him to look directly into her eyes. "Do you trust me, Scott?"

"Yes."

"Then trust me when I say we need to get you to the hospital."

"You'll be there?"

"Of course."

"Okay."

* * *

A few hours later Bree sat in the waiting area hoping for good news about Scott's condition. Physically he was uninjured. His walking challenges seemed to be more about coordination than an injury to his legs. And the way they'd found him... It had looked as though he'd randomly decided to take a nap in the forest.

Strange, since she assumed he'd gone out there to collect more evidence in the tainted water case. She'd ask him about the samples when he regained some clarity.

Because when they found him, Scott seemed disoriented and foggy. He didn't say much on the hike back to the car, or on the way to the E.R.

It was almost as if his personality was absent, that he was a blank slate, although he was still determined about wanting Bree to stay close.

Harvey walked up to her carrying two cups. He offered her one. "Got you some tea."

"Thanks."

"What do you think?" he asked.

"About?"

"Your guy in there. He didn't seem right."

"I hope it's not more head trauma," she whispered.

Harvey sat down next to her. "No sense making it worse than it is. Let's wait and see what the doctors say."

She nodded, sipping her hot tea.

Out of the corner of her eye she spotted Uncle Chuck headed her way. "Breanna, what brings you to the E.R.?" he asked.

"A friend."

"Scott Becket?"

"Actually, yes."

"What's he done now?"

"What are you doing at the hospital, Uncle Chuck?" she redirected.

"Getting my gunshot wound checked out," he said, cradling his arm. "Thought I might have ripped the stitches."

"Oh, no, are you okay?" she asked.

"He's tough, right, Chief?" Harvey said.

Chuck frowned at Harvey. "I'm fine. But now that I see Breanna is here I'm worried."

"About?" She leaned back in her chair and sipped her tea.

"Aren't you tired of E.R.'s?"

"Actually, they've got pretty good tea." She smiled, not wanting to argue with Chuck about her being here for Scott.

"Breanna McBride?" a nurse called from the examining area.

"That would be me." Bree stood and brushed past Chuck to the nurse.

"Scott is asking for you." She motioned Bree into the examining area.

Uncle Chuck tried going with her, but the nurse stopped him. "I'm sorry, sir, just Breanna."

"I'm here if you need me," Chuck offered.

"Thanks," she said and followed the nurse. As Bree approached Scott's bed, he reached out for her. She took his hand and gave it a comforting squeeze.

"Hey," she said. "You scared us."

"Sorry." He glanced at their entwined hands.

"Don't be sorry. I'm glad you're okay." She looked at the doctor. "He's okay, right? No further head trauma?"

"No, although we weren't sure at first because of his impaired cognitive function. I'm running some blood tests to see what's in his system."

"Oh, okay," Bree said, perplexed. Scott hardly took pain relievers for his headaches. Why would the doctors think he was on drugs?

"The doctor says I can go," Scott said.

"Actually, what I said was I'd like to keep him overnight for observation, but I won't force the issue," the doctor said.

"Scott, if the doctor thinks—"

"I want to go home, Breanna. Take me home."

"To Chicago?"

"To the resort."

She studied their hands.

"Unless you don't want me there," he said.

"I have another patient," the doctor said. "I'd advise keeping an eye on Mr. Becket for twenty-four hours."

"Of course," Bree said.

The doctor disappeared on the other side of the curtain.

"It's okay," Scott said, "I understand if you'd rather keep your distance."

"Don't say that. You know how I feel about you."

"But?"

"Your girlfriend showing up kind of threw me off."

"Ex-girlfriend."

"So it's true?" she asked. "You remembered?"

"Remembered what?"

"Your sister called looking for you and said you and Christa broke up last month."

"Then why would Christa…?" He hesitated and frowned. "Oh."

"What?"

"If there are drugs in my system, they got there because of Christa."

"How did that happen?"

"I told her I was heading up into the mountains and she insisted I take her water bottle. If it was laced with something that means she's working with whoever is after me and the evidence. Wow, they even got to her." He leaned back against the pillow. "I don't know which end is up anymore."

"Hey—" she touched his cheek and he opened his eyes "—take a breath." They took a breath together, then another one. "It's okay. I'm taking you home and we'll figure the rest of this out."

* * *

When they got to Scott's hotel room, Bree suggested he stay at her cottage for the day so she could observe his behavior.

"It's not necessary," he said, going through the chest of drawers looking for something. He couldn't remember what.

"I have to insist," she said. "You shouldn't be alone." Her phone vibrated and she snapped it off her belt. "What is the deal today?"

"What's wrong?"

"Another missing hiker."

"You should go."

"I'm not leaving you."

"There's only a few hours of daylight left. They probably need as many volunteers as possible."

She sighed. "You're right. But would you please wait at my cottage for me to get back?"

"Okay." He pulled her into a hug and held on for a few seconds, then released her, looking down into her beautiful green eyes. "Be careful," he said and kissed her. The way she leaned into him, welcoming the gesture, made him feel confident and at peace. When he broke the kiss, she glanced up and smiled.

"That was nice," she said.

"I'm glad you think so."

She gave him the security code and key to her place. "See you later?"

"Yes, ma'am."

After she left he headed to her cottage, hyperaware of his surroundings. But he didn't see anything strange like "Rich" hiding in the bushes. Scott climbed her front steps, pressed the code and went inside.

He hesitated beside the living room, now decorated for Christmas. He could picture her there, surrounded by friends, opening presents and drinking hot apple cider. A smile tugged at his lips.

He wished they'd met under normal circumstances, through mutual friends or church. Scott realized for once he considered going to church if he knew he'd meet Breanna there.

"Stop dreaming," he muttered and headed to the kitchen where she kept her laptop. He wanted to open the map program again, the one that showed a direct line between Lake Hawthorne, the GRI plant and the river where he'd taken a sample yesterday. He tapped his jeans pocket. The vial was still safe and sound.

A knock at the front door echoed down the hallway. Bree must have forgotten something and she couldn't get into the house because she'd given Scott her key. He went to the front door and swung it open with a smile.

And was looking at his boss from Chicago.

SEVENTEEN

"Mr. Oppenheimer, what are you doing here?"

"Good, so you remember me," he joked. "And please, call me Phillip. I'm not that much older than you."

Scott motioned him inside.

"I was in Seattle on business and heard you were in Echo Mountain so I thought I'd track you down," Phillip said.

"How did you know where to find me?"

"The concierge said if you weren't in your room you might be visiting a friend in this quaint cottage. I don't suppose she's got a coffeemaker back there?" He glanced down the hallway to the kitchen.

"Of course." Scott led him back to the kitchen, stunned that the man cared enough to come looking for Scott.

"I'm a bit shocked you're here." Scott

motioned to the kitchen table and his boss sat down.

Scott brewed coffee, realizing how odd it felt to be in Bree's kitchen having a conversation with his boss from Chicago. It was as though he was straddling two different worlds.

"I understand you suffered a head injury and have amnesia?" Phillip said.

"Yes, sir, but I'm starting to remember. I think I've found solid evidence of sabotage."

"Excellent."

"I believe someone has been dumping illegal toxins from the plant into natural water sources in the Cascades, then made it look like the plant was responsible," Scott said.

"Yes, and I suspect I know who's behind it," Phillip said.

"You do?" Scott poured two mugs of coffee and slid one to Phillip.

"A competitor from South America," Phillip said. "I actually resolved this issue a month ago."

"But then why did you send me up here?"

"To finish closing the plant. Then you fell off the grid and I sent someone else."

"But men have been after me."

"Probably the saboteurs hoping to stop you from destroying evidence."

"Destroying evidence? I don't understand."

"That came out wrong." He leaned back in his chair. "You were going to supervise the dissemination of equipment and ship it to a new, more secure location in Idaho."

"This was all for nothing?"

"No, Scott. Whatever evidence you have I can take to the feds and clear our company of any wrongdoing. I'd like to get on that as quickly as possible."

Scott hesitated, but realized this was his boss, the man he was trying to protect.

He dug the vial out of his pocket. "I took this water sample yesterday from a river between the plant and Lake Hawthorne."

"Good, excellent," Phillip said, taking the vial.

Scott considered telling him about the two vials he'd given to someone for safekeeping, but since Scott couldn't remember who had them he decided to keep it to himself so he wouldn't look like an idiot.

"The men who are after me and my friend Breanna—"

"Should leave you alone once I meet with authorities," Phillip said.

"And they were after me because…?"

"They wanted to stop you from gathering evidence that would clear my name. I have some evidence of my own. I'll be going to the feds and ending this within the next twenty-four hours thanks to you." He held up the vial. "You should be very proud of yourself."

"Thank you, sir," Scott said, but for some reason he didn't feel proud. Perhaps because he'd put Bree in the line of fire.

"My senior advisors were concerned about your behavior, but I said you'd come through in the end. Well, I'd better get going. My jet's waiting at Sea-Tac."

Scott walked his boss down the hallway and opened the door.

"Why don't you take another week to recuperate?" Phillip said. "It's invigorating out here."

"Thank you, sir."

They shook hands.

Scott's gaze caught on Phillip's gold, chain link bracelet. A flash of memory rushed through his mind: Phillip slamming his fist on a desk.

Leave it alone, Becket!

But if someone's illegally dumping—

They're not and that's the end of it.

For Scott, it had only been the beginning. Scott ripped his hand from Phillip's.

This man was the enemy.

"Scott?" Phillip questioned.

Now what? If Scott revealed his thoughts, this could go bad awfully fast. Phillip traveled with security, Scott knew that firsthand since he'd been one of them. Security had to be close, waiting for Phillip's signal to swoop in and neutralize the threat—Scott.

"I get these random migraines," Scott said, rubbing his temples for effect.

"From your fall in the mountains?"

"Yes, sir."

"It's a good thing they have a well-trained search and rescue group in Echo County or your injuries might have been much worse." Phillip scanned the mountain range in the distance, then pinned Scott with a serious frown. "Have any of the volunteers ever been hurt while on a mission?"

"Not that I know of."

"That's remarkable considering the rugged nature of the Cascade Mountains. There was commotion in the lobby when I arrived today. Apparently a team was assembling for a mission?"

"Yes, sir."

"Let's hope they all come back unharmed."

Was that a veiled threat?

"They're well trained and experienced," Scott said. "They know what they're doing."

"Yes, but with sudden weather changes I've heard anything could happen." Phillip glanced into Bree's house. "It would be a shame if this lovely girl got caught up in a storm she didn't anticipate." He looked back at Scott. "Wouldn't it?"

So Phillip knew about Breanna. Scott struggled to maintain his self-control, but felt his fingers curl into a fist.

His boss, this entitled, wealthy bully was threatening Breanna in order to keep Scott in line. Had Phillip sent his own men into the mountains as a fail-safe, a way to make sure Scott stayed out of his business? Scott realized that Phillip must have known about the toxic dumping and did nothing to stop it because it would affect the bottom line.

The whole competitor from South America story was a lie.

"Scott?" Phillip snapped his fingers in Scott's face and Scott glanced at him.

"Thought I'd lost you there for a minute," Phillip said.

"I'm sorry, sir. I guess I need to lie down."

"Of course. Give me a call when you're ready to return to work." With a victorious smile, Phillip turned and walked to a waiting limousine. "Rich" stood beside it wearing a smirk.

Scott shut the door, paralyzed by the thought of Bree being vulnerable and in danger while on a mission because Phillip's men were sent to hurt her if Scott pointed the finger at the real criminal: Phillip Oppenheimer.

"No," he ground out, as a rush of memory flooded to the surface. He hadn't taken time off to investigate Phillip's enemies, he'd taken time off to prove his theory about Phillip being responsible for the water contamination. Unfortunately Scott had been assaulted in the mountains before he could get the final water samples to authorities.

And now he'd just handed crucial evidence

over to the enemy. There wasn't time to get another water sample, not with Bree's life at stake, yet he needed something to neutralize Phillip.

If only he had another sample to turn over to authorities. He fisted his hand, struggling with a memory of who he'd given two vials to for safe keeping.

"Later," he said. Right now he had to protect Breanna, but he couldn't do it alone.

Ten minutes later Aiden showed up at Bree's cottage.

"What's the emergency?" Aiden said, stepping inside.

Scott scanned the area and shut the door. "Your sister's in trouble."

"She's been in trouble ever since you fell at her feet, what else is new?" He went into the kitchen and poured himself a cup of coffee.

"My boss from Chicago was here," Scott said. "I'm pretty sure he's behind the tainted water. He's the one who sent the muscle to neutralize me, and now he's threatening Bree."

"You're being paranoid. He doesn't even know her." Aiden sipped his coffee.

"He's using Bree to keep me from talking to the authorities."

"Bree's with Harvey on a mission. She's fine."

"Don't you understand, he's probably sent his men out there in case I did something stupid. He's a manipulative, dangerous man!"

Aiden raised an eyebrow at Scott as though he was questioning Scott's sanity.

"Look, Aiden, I'll do anything, even promise to stay away from your sister if you'd just take me seriously. Please—" his voice cracked "—you've got to help me protect her."

Aiden cocked his head as if he were putting together a puzzle. "What do you want me to do?"

"Call field command and tell them not to let Bree go on the mission, say there's a family emergency or something. Then go get her and keep her safe."

"What about you?"

"I have to figure out where I stashed the other evidence. I left it with someone but can't remember who."

"Bree's gonna be upset when I pull her off the mission."

"As long as she's safe, she can be furious."

Scott spent the next hour in Harvey's office going through video footage of the resort, hoping to see something that could give him a clue as to where he'd hidden the two vials. They were critical in his investigation; he wouldn't have given them to just anyone.

But he wouldn't have involved the cops, not until he was sure he had enough evidence against Phillip.

Nervous energy drove him to check messages at the front desk, hoping for one from Aiden about Bree being back and safe at the resort.

"Hello, Mr. Becket," a young man in his twenties said from behind the counter. His nametag read Tripp.

"Hi, I'm wondering if anyone's left any messages for me?"

The clerk checked Scott's box. "Nothing up here, but they could have left a message in your room's voice mail."

"Thanks." He started for his room.

"Mr. Becket?" Tripp said.

Scott turned to him.

"They're serving Baked Alaska for dessert in the dining room tonight."

Scott narrowed his eyes at the guy. "Okay, thanks."

"Baked Alaska," the clerk repeated with a nod.

Scott walked back to the front desk. "And you're telling me this because…?"

"Tripp, do you know if—" Nia hesitated as she came out of the office. "Oh, sorry, I didn't realize you were with a guest. How are you feeling, Mr. Becket?"

"Better, thanks." He glanced at Tripp. "Baked Alaska, huh?"

"Made it two hours ago."

"Tripp, what are you talking about?" Nia said.

Scott figured Tripp was communicating in code, assuming Scott would understand the message.

"Have you got a minute?" he asked Tripp, and motioned him out from behind the counter.

"Can you watch the desk for a sec?" Tripp asked Nia.

Nia raised an eyebrow. "Sure."

Tripp joined Scott in the lobby and they found a secluded alcove near the coffee station.

"I guess you haven't heard, I had a fall and I'm struggling with my memory," Scott said.

"Whoa, when did that happen?"

"Sunday."

"Ah, I was on vacation until today."

"And the Baked Alaska comment?"

"You asked me to hold something for you in the hotel safe and if anyone inquired about it to let you know by saying *Baked Alaska.*"

"Someone asked about it two hours ago?"

"Yes, sir. He said by chance were you keeping anything in the hotel safe? I was going to tell him I'm not at liberty to share information about our guests, but he looked sketchy so I denied that you'd kept anything with us."

"But there is something there?"

Tripp nodded.

"Man, you might have just saved my life. Can you get it and meet me in the men's bathroom?"

"Sure."

Scott went to the men's room and waited. It seemed more secluded than the public lobby, a better place for the exchange. A few minutes later Tripp entered the bathroom and handed Scott a padded envelope.

"Thanks," Scott said.

"Of course. If you need anything else, I work the day shift." With a nod Tripp left and Scott studied the package.

This was it. At least he hoped this was it—the evidence he'd hidden before his hike up into the mountains.

He ripped open the envelope exposing two vials of liquid with OPR and SR, which stood for Oppenheimer Plant Reservoir and Susha River. Bingo. Both were bodies of water that, if tainted, proved the toxins were coming directly from Phillip's plant. Scott also found a flash drive inside the envelope.

"Huh." He shoved the drive into his jeans pocket and slipped the vials into his jacket. It was all coming together.

Anxious to see what was on the flash drive, Scott walked through the lobby heading back to Bree's cottage. He'd use her laptop to access the information.

As he turned the corner, he spotted Bree's uncle Chuck hovering in the hallway.

"Chief?" Scott said.

"Where have you been? She's been asking for you."

"Who, Bree?"

"Come on." He motioned Scott down the hall.

"Is she okay? Why didn't Aiden call?"

"Now not, not now," he hushed.

Panic knotted in Scott's chest. Had she been hurt? Was Aiden too late?

They went outside and her uncle motioned Scott toward his police cruiser.

"Where is she?" Scott said.

"Stop talking and get in."

Something felt off.

"Hang on, where is Bree?"

"I said, get in!" Uncle Chuck withdrew his firearm and pointed it at Scott's chest. "You wouldn't leave her alone. You had to involve her in this garbage."

He flicked the gun barrel toward the car. Scott knew he wasn't being taken to see Bree. He also knew if he got into the car, he wasn't getting out alive.

"Get in or I'll shoot you where you stand," the man threatened.

"Uncle Chuck, what are you doing?" Bree gasped.

EIGHTEEN

Bree couldn't believe her uncle was threatening to shoot Scott.

"It's his fault, all of this is his fault," Uncle Chuck said in a tight voice she didn't recognize.

"What's his fault?" Bree asked, stepping into his sight line, hoping to dissuade him.

"All this violence is because this man came to Echo Mountain."

"No, the men who were after Scott are responsible for the violence."

"Because of him!" he shouted.

Aiden jogged up behind Uncle Chuck and she put out her hand to caution him to stay back. Her uncle was having some kind of breakdown and she didn't want him to be startled into pulling the trigger.

"Why don't you lower the gun and we'll talk about it?" Bree suggested.

"No more talking." He flicked the barrel of the gun at Scott. "He's got what I want. Let's have it."

Scott pulled something out of his jacket pocket and held it up. Two vials of liquid.

"Give it to me. I'm taking it to the feds and I'll end this thing."

"It's dangerous to have these in your possession," Scott said.

"I can handle this alone."

"But you shouldn't have to," Bree said. "That's what family and friends are for, to help each other fight the hard battles."

He glanced at her with misty eyes and she thought she might have gotten through to him.

Instead, he redirected his attention to Scott. "The vials."

Scott placed them on the ground.

"Back up," Uncle Chuck said.

Scott did as ordered and nodded at Bree to stay back.

Uncle Chuck picked up the vials, but didn't lower the gun. "All this for a little bit of contaminated water."

"How did you know it was contaminated?" Scott said.

"It says so on here." Chuck glanced at the vials.

An odd expression crossed his face, like he'd been caught with his hand in the cookie jar.

"Don't confuse me!" He took a step toward Scott.

Aiden charged Uncle Chuck from behind. The gun went off.

Scott tackled Bree to the ground. Air rushed from her lungs. "Sorry, you okay?" he said.

She nodded, unable to verbally respond as she gasped for breath.

"Let go of me!" Uncle Chuck shouted.

"Drop the gun!" Aiden countered.

"Stay down," Scott said into Bree's ear and slid off of her.

Bree stayed down all right, she stayed down and prayed. Prayed that no one would be hurt and that Uncle Chuck would come down from whatever anxiety spin he was on.

She also hoped she'd misinterpreted Chuck's reaction and he wasn't part of the master plan to poison the natural water sources in the area. But that's what Scott had implied, right?

Another shot rang out and she gasped.

"The gun," Aiden said.

"Got it."

"Relax, Uncle Chuck," Aiden ordered.

Bree heard the sound of a man sobbing. She glanced to her right. Chuck was chest down with Aiden's knee pressed against his back.

"If I let you go, will you be okay?" Aiden said. "No crazy stuff?"

Uncle Chuck nodded. Aiden helped him sit up.

Scott crouched beside Uncle Chuck. "You knew about the illegal dumping, didn't you?"

He didn't answer.

"I'll call 9-1-1." Aiden stood and pulled out his phone.

Bree kneeled beside Scott. "Uncle Chuck, what's going on?"

Chuck stared blindly toward the mountains. "He said he was going to clean it up, build another plant, employ thousands of locals."

"Did he pay you—" Scott hesitated "—for your cooperation?"

"Do you know how little a municipal police chief makes?" He glanced at Bree. "I wanted to propose to your mom and take her on a nice honeymoon to Greece."

"So you allowed Phillip Oppenheimer to break the law?" Scott said.

Chuck glared at Scott. "Get me a lawyer."

Bree touched Chuck's shoulder and he glanced at her with bloodshot eyes. "Why did you have to find him out there?" he said softly. "He was never supposed to come down from the mountain."

"They're on the way," Aiden said, eyeing Chuck. "I don't get it. You're involved with poisoning your own town, your friends... Mom?"

Uncle Chuck looked away.

"Sometimes money and power are too hard to resist," Scott offered. "Especially when served up by a master manipulator like Phillip Oppenheimer."

Bree spent three hours at the police station giving her statement, first to Chief Washburn, then to federal officers who were taking over the case. Apparently illegal dumping wasn't the only crime committed by the powerful Phillip Oppenheimer, but the feds hadn't been able to charge him with anything else to date.

As she sat in a chair by the chief's desk she felt emotionally and physically exhausted. The most draining part of the day had been the few minutes when she thought her uncle might shoot and kill Scott.

"Hey," Scott said, placing a hand on her shoulder. "It's over."

She glanced up at him. He looked different for some reason, distant, and a little bit like a stranger.

"What about the men who are after you, me, us?" she said.

"Federal officers are detaining Phillip Oppenheimer and his men at the airport," Scott said. "Apparently the flash drive I gave them has plenty of evidence, including emails and voice mails, proving Phillip knew about the toxins."

"Looks like the feds have identified the dead man from the plant as one of Oppenheimer's security agents," Chief Washburn said, walking up to them. "From what we can piece together, Chuck shot him because he threatened to kidnap you, Breanna, thinking you'd be good leverage to control Scott.

They were trying to discredit Scott by planting the gun, making the petty cash accusation, among other things. Why was your girlfriend involved?"

"Ex-girlfriend," Scott corrected. "I'd suspected she was on their payroll but couldn't be sure."

"Awfully convenient to have a drugged water bottle in her car before you headed up into the mountains," the chief said.

"She would have drugged me regardless. Another way to make me look mentally unstable so no one would take my claims seriously."

"And the tainted water?" she asked.

"The water council will work on how to purify it before it hits our faucets," the chief said.

Breanna shook her head.

"What?" Scott said.

"I'm having a hard time differentiating between the good guys and bad guys. I mean, Uncle Chuck?"

"That surprised me, too," Chief Washburn said. "But Oppenheimer made promises, convinced Chuck he had big plans for the area. If he'd followed through on those promises, Chuck would have certainly come out the hero."

"Why did Uncle Chuck believe him?"

"Because it's easier to believe you're doing the right thing than to admit you're a part of the problem," Scott offered.

Bree sensed he wasn't talking about Chuck. But why would Scott take on so much personal responsibility about his boss's plans? Scott was trying to bring justice to the situation.

"Can I talk to you outside for a second?" she said to Scott.

"They might need me—"

"I'll let them know where you are," Chief Washburn said.

"Okay, thanks."

Bree took Scott's hand and led him out front. The town's decorations illuminated the street with multicolored bells, stars and snowflakes hanging from streetlights. She smiled at the sight.

Scott slid his hand from hers and she studied him with a heavy heart. She feared what was coming next, so she tried a diversion.

"Isn't it beautiful?"

He shoved his hands into his jacket pockets and glanced down the street, the lights reflecting in his eyes. She was sure he wasn't seeing the beauty of the display as she just had.

"Why do I get the feeling you were talking about yourself when you said it's easier to believe a lie than to believe you're part of the problem?" she asked.

He clenched his jaw.

"Come on, talk to me."

He glanced up. The intensity of his gaze shot a chill to her core.

"It's the truth," he said. "I was a part of the problem."

"You were trying to fix the problem."

"I involved innocent people in the process. Someone could have gotten hurt. You could have been hurt."

"But I wasn't. It's over and everything's okay."

He shook his head. "Chuck was right about one thing—I continually put you in danger."

"Scott, it was those men—"

"If I hadn't asked, make that begged you to stay by me that first night at the hospital you wouldn't have been in danger."

"You were alone and you needed my help."

"Well, I don't anymore."

She tried covering the pain arcing across her chest with a sigh. "It's okay to need someone, Scott."

"Not for me it isn't. I take care of people, I don't put them in the line of fire, like that kid...." He shook his head.

"Miguel?"

He stared at the ground.

"Why do you blame yourself for his death?"

"Because he was killed trying to help me. I didn't ask him to," he said, his voice sounding raw as he spoke. "I told him to stay out of it, that I'd nail the gang for his brother's murder and instead he ends up dead, too."

"He was trying to do the right thing. That was his choice. Not yours."

"It was my fault. If I would have closed the case faster he wouldn't have gone snooping around."

"Scott, we can't take responsibility for other people's choices. I made the choice to help you at the hospital and nothing was going to change my mind. My choice." She took a chance and placed her hand over his heart. "And I'm glad I did."

"Why?" he whispered. "I've got nothing to offer you, no job, no future."

"Hey, we just survived a life-threatening situation. Let's enjoy the moment and not worry about the future."

"I can't help it," he said with incredible sadness in his voice. "I need to know you're going to be happy."

"I'm happy right now." She slid her arms around his waist and looked up at him. "The lights are beautiful and hope is in the air. Mom's open house is tomorrow night and the Christmas tree lighting ceremony is—"

"No." He removed her arms from his waist and looked into her eyes. "This is your world, Breanna, not mine. I come from a violent world and will not infect you with that ugliness."

"Scott—"

He interrupted her protest with a kiss. It was gentle, warm and filled with desperation.

It was a goodbye kiss.

Tears formed in her eyes. Somehow this man didn't think himself worthy of happiness and love.

He broke the kiss and hugged her. "You are...incredible."

He released her and bolted into the police station.

Bree stood there for a few minutes, unsure what to do next. Should she follow him? Confront him with the truth that he was, in fact, worthy of love? Probably not a good idea in front of a room full of law enforcement officials.

She sensed that nothing she said would change his mind. Somehow he'd have to find enlightenment on his own. Well, not totally alone.

Please, God, help him see he is worthy of Your love.

Glancing up at the dark sky dotted with stars, she considered her next move. Instinct told her to give him space.

But she wouldn't let him leave Echo Mountain without giving him one last gift.

The next day Aiden showed up unannounced at Scott's room to check up on him. Scott hadn't heard from Bree since their conversation in front of the police station.

And the kiss. Scott closed his eyes at the memory of her soft, perfect lips.

"Let me get this straight, my sister helped you out this past week and you're going to leave without saying goodbye?" Aiden said, leaning against the wall, eating an apple. "That's harsh."

"It's better that way."

"Better for...?"

Scott glanced at Aiden. "Her."

"Oh, okay," Aiden said, disbelief coloring his voice. "You still have one more thing to do before you leave town."

"The feds said I could go back to Chicago."

"Not the feds, my mother. She wants you to stop by her Christmas open house tonight. And trust me, you don't want to turn her down."

"I've got a plane to catch."

"Really? After everything you put that woman through?"

Scott glanced at Aiden.

"You practically got her daughter killed," Aiden said. "Then you expose Mom's boy-friend as a criminal."

"So she wants me to come by her party to rip me in front of the whole town?"

Aiden shrugged. "Doubt it. She's about compassion and forgiveness, kind of like Bree."

Bree's compassion had astonished Scott on more than one occasion.

"Are you going to rejoin the force when you get back to Chicago?" Aiden asked.

"I don't know. My heart's not in it."

"Yeah, chucklehead, I know where your heart is," Aiden said.

"I promised you I'd stay away from Bree."

"Hey, don't make me the bad guy here." Aiden pushed away from the wall. "I'm starting to think it's not the worst idea in the world, I mean, you and my sister."

"You're messing with me," Scott said, eyeing Aiden.

"No, I'm not. Bree couldn't trust guys after being with that jerk, Thomas. Then you literally fell at her feet and something changed. Maybe because you were vulnerable and needy, I don't know. But my sister's grown a ton this past week thanks to you. She's got her groove back." Aiden smiled.

"I'm glad." He stuffed a sweatshirt into his duffel bag. "I'm really glad."

"And you really love her."

Scott hesitated as he rolled up his jeans. "It doesn't matter."

"If love doesn't matter then what does?"

Aiden's words haunted him, but Scott knew he was doing the right thing. Letting Breanna go was the true act of love. She'd be free to find another, better man with whom to spend her life.

Scott climbed the steps leading to Mrs. McBride's front porch and reached for the door.

"I wasn't sure you'd come."

He spun around and spotted Bree, bundled up in a fleece blanket, sitting on the porch swing.

"Aiden said not to refuse your mom so…"

"Oh." Bree glanced down.

He instantly regretted his words. He should have said he needed to see Bree one more time, drink in the sight of her face so he'd never forget it.

"I have something for you." She unfolded her legs and grabbed a gift bag from the floor. "It's an emergency kit with everything you need in case you get stuck in the mountains again."

"Thanks."

"Open it."

Scott wandered to a chair and sat down. Excitement danced in her eyes as she watched him. He'd miss that, too, her enthusiasm.

The kit had all the essentials including matches in a plastic bag, a headlamp, pocketknife, mini-first-aid kit, sunscreen, freeze-dried food and a flashlight. Hooked to the flashlight was a key chain that read: *Let Go, Let God*.

"Nice touch." He smiled.

"You'll have to supply the extra clothes and shelter."

"Shelter, even on a day hike?"

"You never know what you'll encounter in the mountains."

Their eyes caught. No, he couldn't have known he'd find the love of his life in the Cascade Mountains.

"There should be one more thing." She smiled, expectant.

He dug into the bag and pulled out a compass. "So I won't get lost, nice."

"Flip it over," she said.

He turned the compass over and on the

back was a photo of Bree and Fiona. "Wow, this is great," he said, his heart aching.

"We're always close, Scott. All of us." She went to him and kissed him on the cheek.

He closed his eyes for a second.

And she was gone. The door clicked shut as she disappeared into the house.

His gaze drifted to the photo of Bree and Fiona. How could he leave her?

Aiden was right. Love matters. A lot.

Who would have thought a mind-altering head injury would teach Scott how to trust and love? He'd spent most of his life feeling discarded and unloved. And now, when love was handed to him like a gift, he was going to reject it? That made no sense.

But Breanna did. Everything about her made sense from her gentle way to her determined attitude; her devotion to family and her faith in God.

Leaving Bree would be turning his back on the most amazing thing that had ever happened to him.

He glanced at the key chain attached to the flashlight. "Let Go, Let God," he whispered. He clicked the light on, aimed it across the property and clicked it off. "Show me the way, Lord."

He stuffed the essentials back into the bag and headed for the house, expecting to be shunned by locals and lectured by Bree's mom.

He opened the door and held his breath....

Everyone greeted him as though he were an old friend. Nia handed him a hot apple cider and Grace from the SAR K9 unit offered him a plate of cookies, which he had to put down in order to greet Reverend Charles. The pastor shook Scott's hand and said they could use his help at a fund-raising event next week if Scott was still in town.

Scott felt like a celebrity; he felt as though he belonged.

A new feeling. A good feeling.

Harvey came up beside him and smiled. "Glad you're A-okay."

"Thanks, and thanks for all your help this past week."

"About that—" Harvey hesitated "—I'm worn out from all that horsing around. I need a vacation, or maybe I need to retire, take some trips, go fishing for a week or a year."

Scott chuckled. "Sounds like a plan."

"I don't suppose you'd want to take over as security manager for the resort?"

Scott snapped his attention to Harvey. "You can't offer me your job."

"I didn't, but I think he will." He glanced across the room at Aiden, who cracked a smile and nodded at Scott.

"You mean...?"

"He's willing to give you a trial run while I'm still around to supervise. But let me know in the next 48 hours or else we'll post an ad in the *Echo Mountain Review*."

"Don't post the ad," Scott blurted out.

Harvey burst out laughing, slapped Scott on the shoulder and wandered into the crowd.

Scott had never felt the sense of community he did at this very moment; a sense of belonging. He'd always been the lone wolf, the man of the family who needed to take care of his mom and sister, which didn't leave time for making friends or being part of a community.

Yet somehow he'd found himself surrounded by people who cared, thanks to Breanna's family.

Breanna, the woman he loved with all his heart.

A clinking sound hushed the crowd. Everyone quieted and glanced at Bree's mom. "I'd like to publicly thank our guest, Scott Becket, for exposing the toxic dumping mess and protecting our community."

The group applauded. He scanned the crowd looking for Bree.

"Thanks to Scott—"

"You're back in the dating pool!" Harvey called out.

Everyone chuckled.

Scott glanced at Mrs. McBride. "I am sorry about that."

"Don't be. I've been wanting to break it off with Chuck for months but didn't have a good reason other than my gut telling me it wasn't right."

"Gotta listen to those gut feelings," Scott said.

Mrs. McBride raised her cup of cider. "To Scott Becket."

The group cheered, smiles spreading across their faces.

"Thanks, thanks everyone," he glanced down, embarrassed.

"Okay, speech time is over. Let's finish eating all this great food," Mrs. McBride said.

Scott turned to search the back of the house, but Bree's mom caught his arm.

"Maybe you should take your own advice about your gut feelings?" She winked.

"Am I that transparent?"

She smiled and drifted into the crowd.

A crowd noticeably absent of Bree. His heart rate sped up at the thought she'd left, that he wouldn't see her again tonight.

He ambled through the group, shaking hands and accepting thanks, making his way toward Aiden, who was talking to Nia.

"I don't think it's a good idea, Aiden," Nia said.

"You worry too much.

"What's not a good idea?" Scott said.

"He wants to build a camp at the top of Echo Mountain for guests," Nia said.

"It would be a great draw for business," Aiden said.

"It's dangerous up there," Nia countered. "The high winds and steep slopes."

Aiden waved her off and redirected his

attention to Scott. "So, you interested in Harvey's job?"

"I am."

"Harvey thinks you're a good fit."

"And what do you think?"

Aiden narrowed his eyes. "We'll see how you do during your probationary period."

"Thanks, and thanks for pointing out the obvious back at the hotel room."

"You mean…?"

"About what matters."

"Anytime buddy, anytime."

"Have you guys seen Bree?" Scott asked.

"I think she went out back to check on Fiona," Aiden said.

"Great, thanks." Scott made his way through the house, smiling at neighbors and friends as he passed, anxious to get outside to find Bree.

He placed the gift bag on top of the fridge as he passed through the kitchen and went out the back door. The crisp winter air filled his lungs and stars sparkled above. He scanned the property and didn't see Bree at first, then he heard her giggling.

Scott followed the glorious sound and

found Bree playing ball toss with Fiona on the side of the house.

"Get it, girl. Go get it!" she called.

"Hey," Scott said.

Bree spun around, startled. She swiped at her cheeks and that's when Scott realized she'd been crying.

"It turns out I won't need the compass," he said, approaching her.

"Yeah, why's that?"

"I've found my way home." He reached for her and pulled her into his arms. "And I don't plan on leaving anytime soon."

She studied him with hope in her eyes.

"Your brother offered me a job and I've decided to take it."

"You mean...?"

"I'm yours, Breanna, as long as you'll have me."

She squealed and wrapped her arms around his neck, kissing him with such joy. Scott lifted her up off the ground and twirled in a circle. She giggled against his lips.

Fiona rushed them, bursting into a round of playful barks. Scott broke the kiss and smiled. For the first time since he could remember, he cracked a genuine, heartfelt smile. Bree glanced up at the sky. Soft snowflakes started to fall, landing on her eyelashes.

"Thank you," she whispered.

"For what?"

"My Christmas wish."

He held her tight, thanking God for the wonderful blessing of love.

* * * * *

Dear Reader,

I've always appreciated the phrase, "Only you can do it, but you can't do it alone." Whether you get your strength from God, friends, family or a combination of all three, it is a blessing to be able to trust someone enough to lean on him or her in times of hardship.

In *Covert Christmas,* Scott is forced to trust Breanna after he's assaulted and loses his memory. Being in a strange town and suspected of being involved in criminal activity, he's both traumatized and terrified. Yet free-spirited Breanna stays by his side to help him through. He's amazed by her tenderness, strength and faith in God.

Breanna, on the other hand, learns to trust her instincts and act on them. She's suffered her share of hardship, especially in the boyfriend department, yet that won't stop her from helping a wounded man who's being pursued by gunmen in the mountains. Her past hardships have made her courageous.

Throughout the course of their story, Breanna and Scott learn they do not have to tackle the challenges of life alone. They are able to embrace the importance of leaning on each other and experience a deep, special kind of trust shared between two people.

I hope you're able to find support in times of hardship, and love when you need it most. Remember, God is love.

Peace,
Hope White

Questions for Discussion

1. Do you think Breanna was foolish to help Scott when she found him being pursued by gunmen in the mountains? Why or why not?

2. Was Bree's family justified in worrying about her becoming attached to Scott? If so, why?

3. Do you think Scott should have tried harder to push Bree away? Why?

4. Why do you think Scott leaned so heavily on Bree?

5. What part of Scott's past do you think haunted him the most?

6. Did you understand Bree not wanting to tell her family about her abusive boyfriend?

7. If Scott and Bree had met under different circumstances, do you think they would have dated?

8. Do you think her brother's overprotectiveness made Bree feel good that someone cared so much, or did it make her feel as though her family didn't believe she could make sensible decisions?

9. How could Scott have worked through the guilt of Miguel's death?

10. How do you think Bree's experience being bullied by her ex-boyfriend helped her motivate Scott to fight?

11. At what point did you suspect Scott was investigating his own boss? What clued you in?

12. Why do you think we sometimes take responsibility for other people's choices?

REQUEST YOUR FREE BOOKS!

2 FREE INSPIRATIONAL NOVELS IN TRUE LARGE PRINT
PLUS 2 FREE MYSTERY GIFTS

YES! Please send me 2 FREE Love Inspired® True Large Print novels and my 2 FREE mystery gifts (gifts are worth about $10). After receiving them, if I don't wish to receive any more books, I can return the shipping statement marked "cancel." If I don't cancel, I will receive 3 brand-new true large print novels every month and be billed just $7.99 per book in the U.S. or $9.99 per book in Canada. That's a savings of at least 20% off the cover price. It's quite a bargain! Shipping and handling is just 50¢ per book in the U.S. and 75¢ per book in Canada.* I understand that accepting the 2 free books and gifts places me under no obligation to buy anything. I can always return the shipment and cancel at any time. Even if I never buy another book, the two free books and gifts are mine to keep forever.

117/317 IDN F5FZ

Name _____ (PLEASE PRINT) _____

Address _____ Apt. # _____

City _____ State/Prov. _____ Zip/Postal Code _____

Signature (if under 18, a parent or guardian must sign)

Mail to the Harlequin® Reader Service:
IN U.S.A.: P.O. Box 1867, Buffalo, NY 14240-1867
IN CANADA: P.O. Box 609, Fort Erie, Ontario L2A 5X3

* Terms and prices subject to change without notice. Prices do not include applicable taxes. Sales tax applicable in N.Y. Canadian residents will be charged applicable taxes. Offer not valid in Quebec. This offer is limited to one order per household. Not valid for current subscribers to Love Inspired True Large Print books. All orders subject to credit approval. Credit or debit balances in a customer's account(s) may be offset by any other outstanding balance owed by or to the customer. Please allow 4 to 6 weeks for delivery. Offer available while quantities last.

Your Privacy—The Harlequin® Reader Service is committed to protecting your privacy. Our Privacy Policy is available online at www.ReaderService.com or upon request from the Harlequin Reader Service.

We make a portion of our mailing list available to reputable third parties that offer products we believe may interest you. If you prefer that we not exchange your name with third parties, or if you wish to clarify or modify your communication preferences, please visit us at www.ReaderService.com/consumerschoice or write to us at Harlequin Reader Service Preference Service, P.O. Box 9062, Buffalo, NY 14269. Include your complete name and address.

LITLP13TRR